PETE BOGG
KING OF THE FROGS

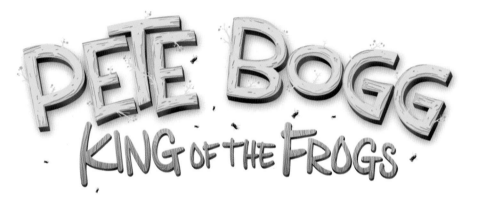

STONE ARCH BOOKS
a capstone imprint

STONE ARCH BOOKS
1710 ROE CREST DRIVE,
NORTH MANKATO, MINNESOTA 56003
WWW.CAPSTONEPUB.COM

CATALOGING-IN-PUBLICATION DATA IS AVAILABLE
ON THE LIBRARY OF CONGRESS WEBSITE.
ISBN (HARDCOVER): 978-1-4342-3284-7
ISBN (PAPERBACK): 978-1-4342-3872-6
ISBN (E-BOOK): 978-1-4342-6096-3

SUMMARY: PETE BOGG HAS LIVED IN THE SWAMPS
HIS WHOLE LIFE. HE'S HAPPY THERE, LIKES THE
FOOD (FLIES), HAS A BEST FRIEND (POLLY WOG),
ENJOYS THE RECREATIONAL ACTIVITIES (LEAP
FROG). HOWEVER, HE'S ALWAYS FELT A LITTLE OUT
OF PLACE. HE WANTS TO FIND HIS REAL PARENTS
AND DISCOVER MORE ABOUT HIS OTHER HALF, HIS
HUMAN HALF. UNFORTUNATELY, THE CITY LIFE FOR A
COUNTRY FROG IS A MIGHTY BIG LEAP.

PRINTED IN THE UNITED STATES IN
STEVENS POINT, WISCONSIN.
092012   006937WZS13

PETE BOGG

KING OF THE FROGS

WRITTEN BY
SCOTT SONNEBORN

ILLUSTRATED BY
**SERGIO MARTINEZ &
ANGÉLICA BRACHO**

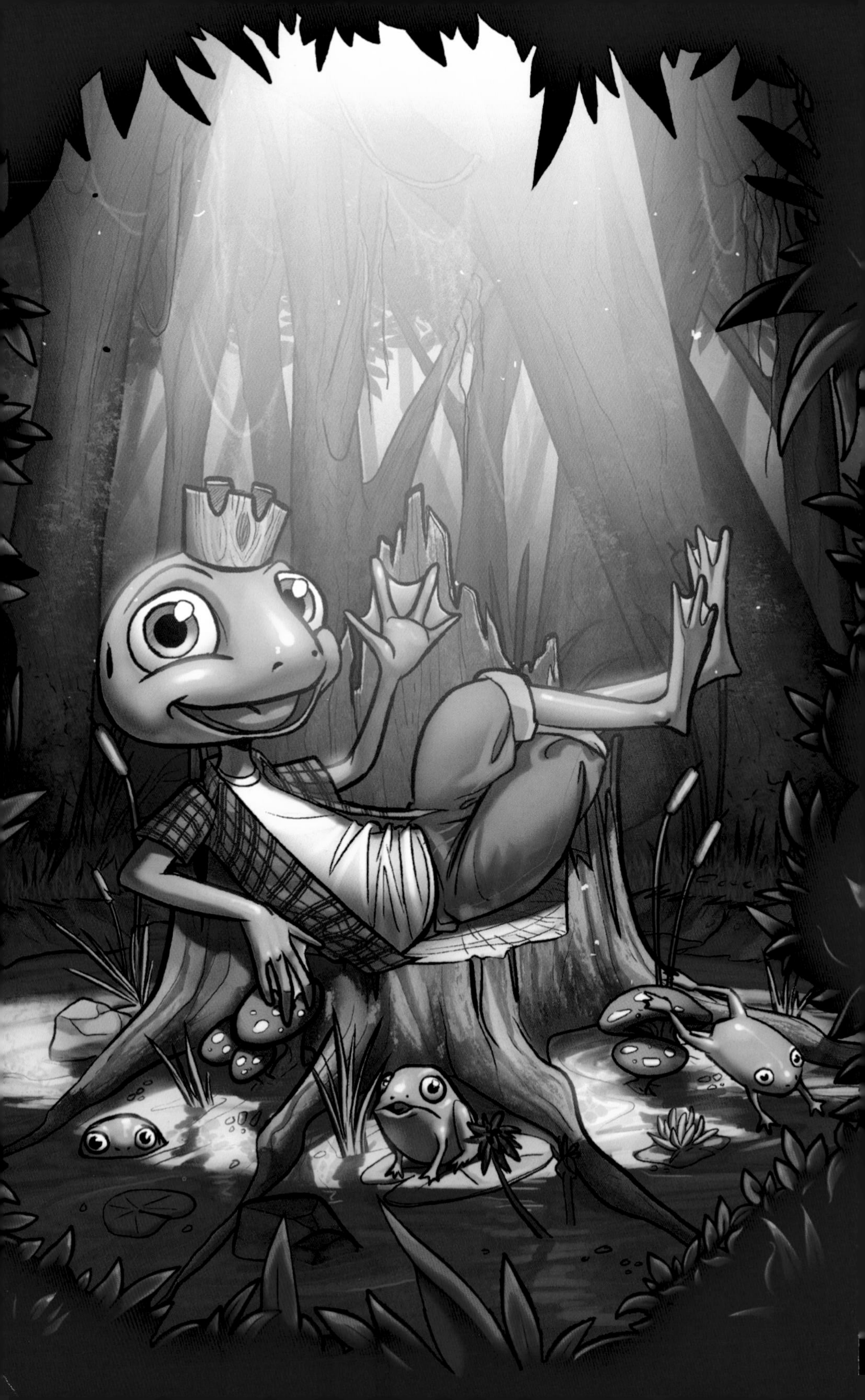

THE TALE OF
PETE BOGG

Once upon a lily pad, a handsome man and beautiful woman fell in love. Soon, this lovely couple married and had a sweet, caring child together. But the handsome man had a deep, dark secret... He was really a frog, temporarily transformed by an evil spell. Why? Well, that's not really important to this story. What is important? The frog-man and his half-frog son fled the city, returning to the swamps to live in peace. And that's where this story begins...

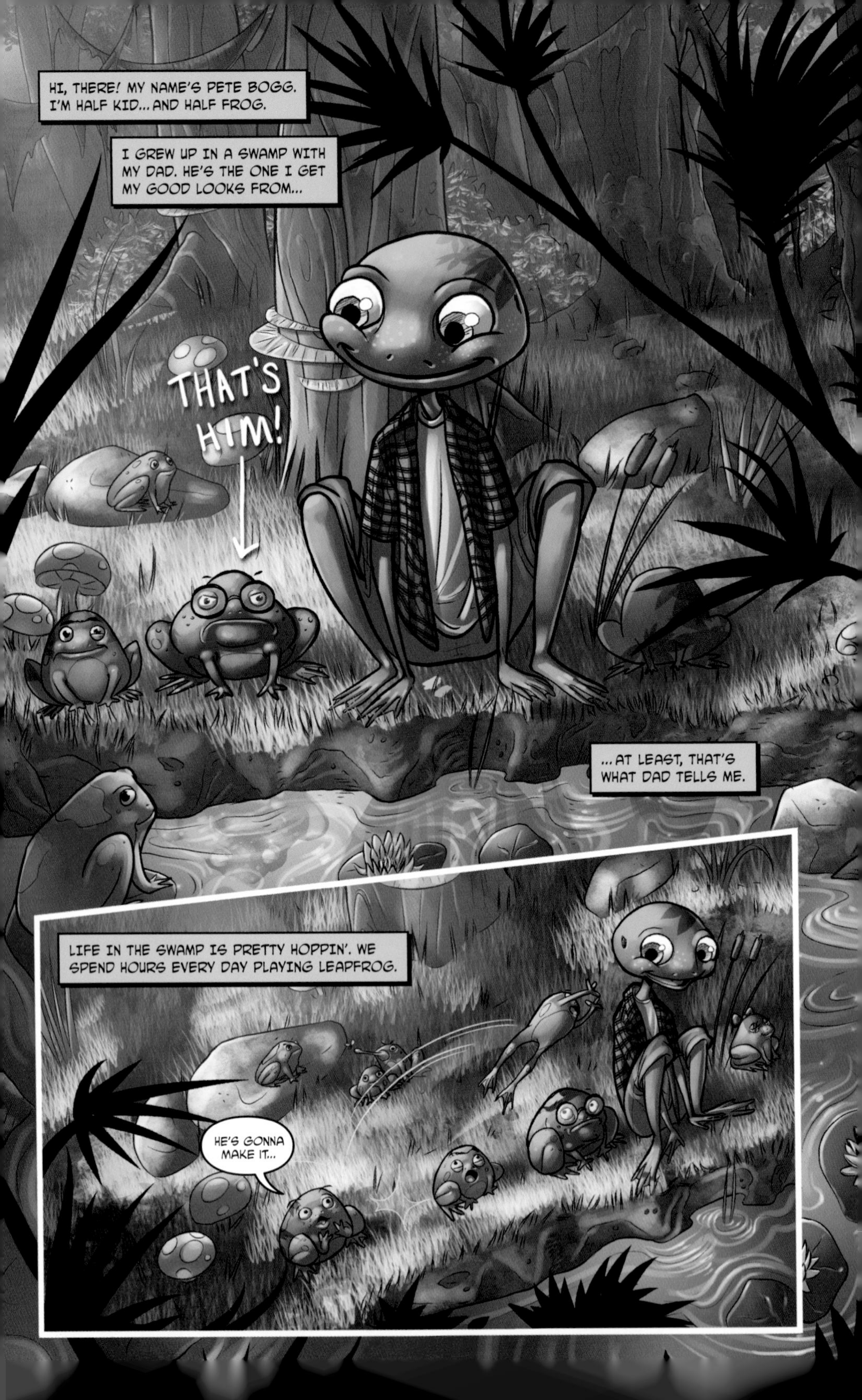
HI, THERE! MY NAME'S PETE BOGG. I'M HALF KID... AND HALF FROG.
I GREW UP IN A SWAMP WITH MY DAD. HE'S THE ONE I GET MY GOOD LOOKS FROM...
THAT'S HIM!
...AT LEAST, THAT'S WHAT DAD TELLS ME.
LIFE IN THE SWAMP IS PRETTY HOPPIN'. WE SPEND HOURS EVERY DAY PLAYING LEAPFROG.
HE'S GONNA MAKE IT...

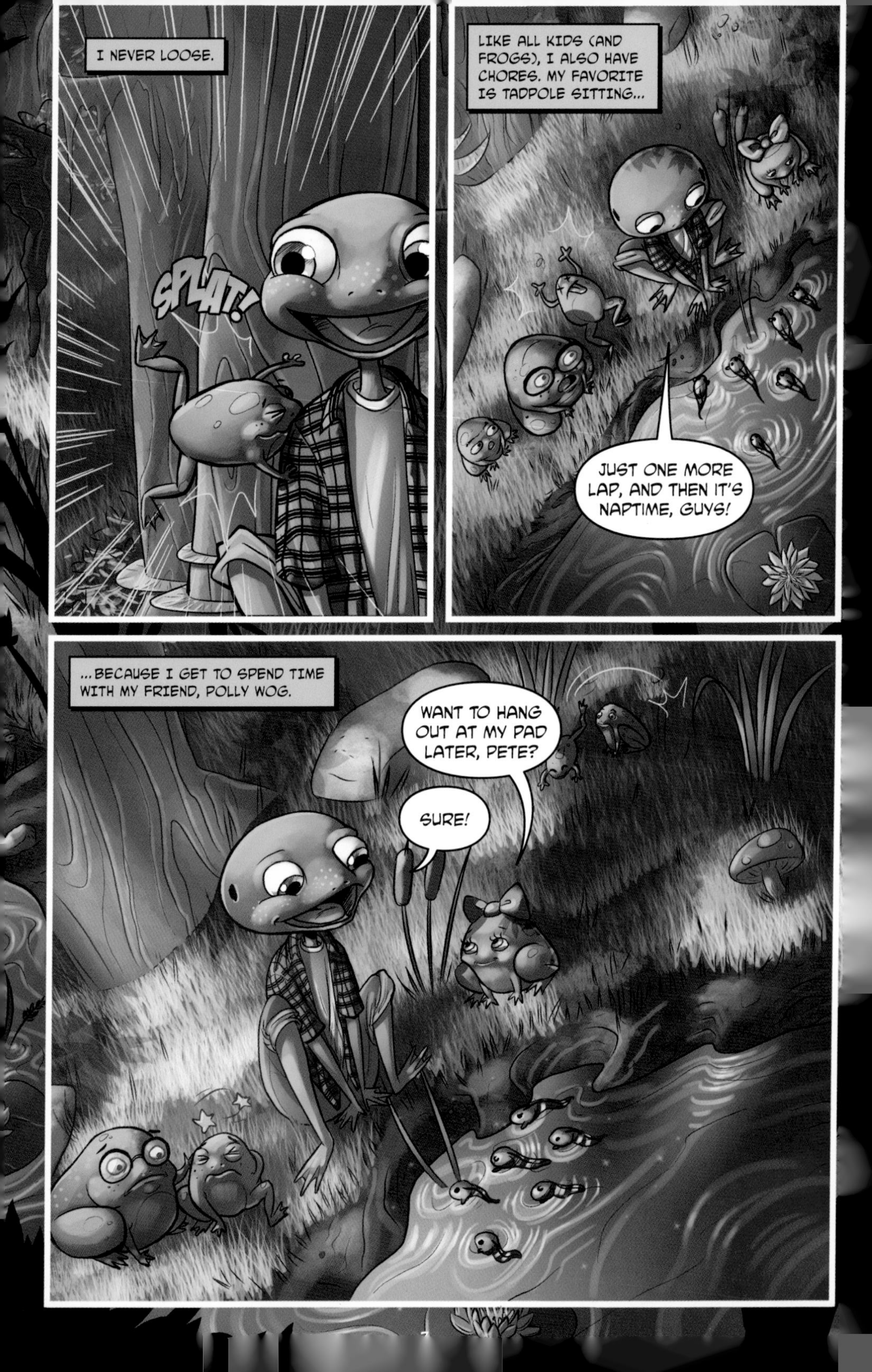
I NEVER LOOSE.
SPLAT!
LIKE ALL KIDS (AND FROGS), I ALSO HAVE CHORES. MY FAVORITE IS TADPOLE SITTING...
JUST ONE MORE LAP, AND THEN IT'S NAPTIME, GUYS!
...BECAUSE I GET TO SPEND TIME WITH MY FRIEND, POLLY WOG.
WANT TO HANG OUT AT MY PAD LATER, PETE?
SURE!

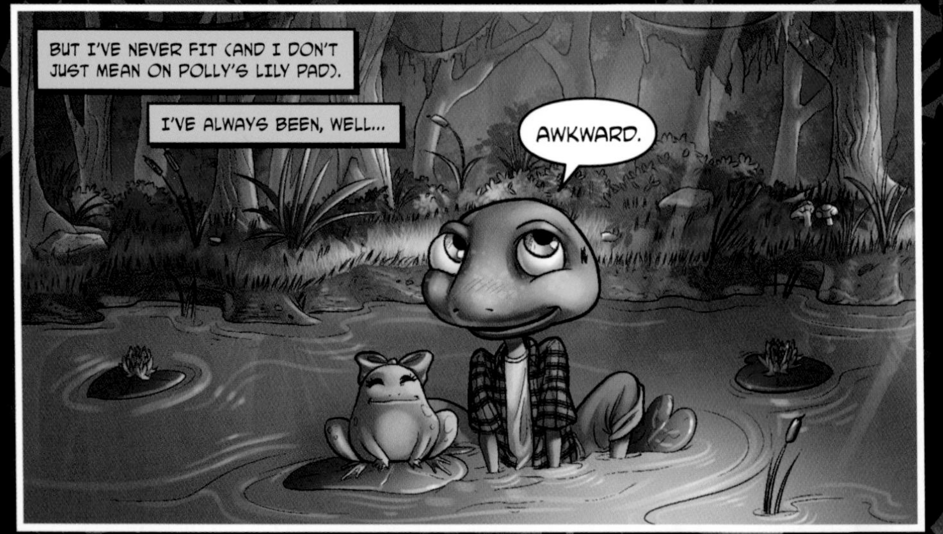
BUT I'VE NEVER FIT (AND I DON'T JUST MEAN ON POLLY'S LILY PAD).
I'VE ALWAYS BEEN, WELL...
AWKWARD.

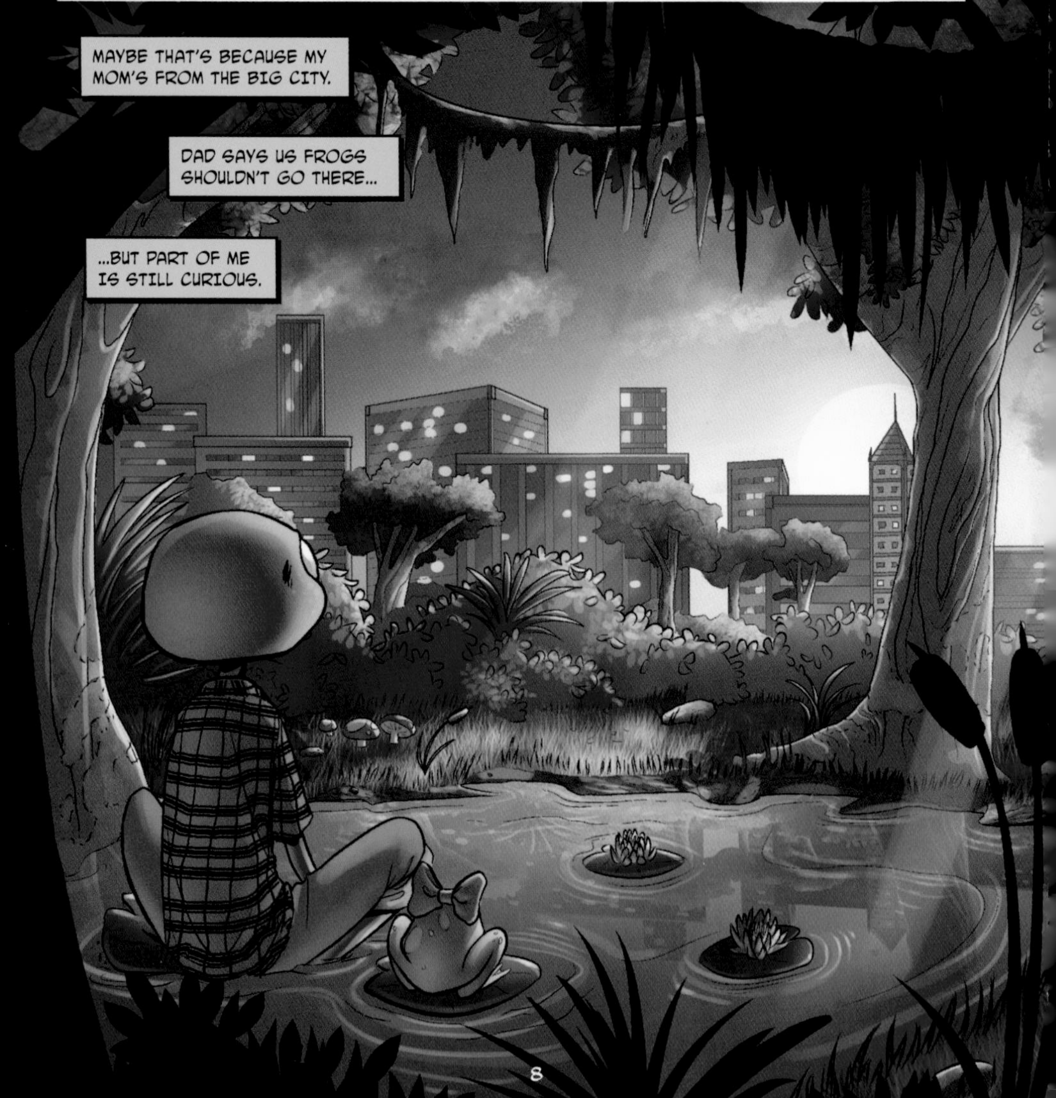
MAYBE THAT'S BECAUSE MY MOM'S FROM THE BIG CITY.
DAD SAYS US FROGS SHOULDN'T GO THERE...
...BUT PART OF ME IS STILL CURIOUS.

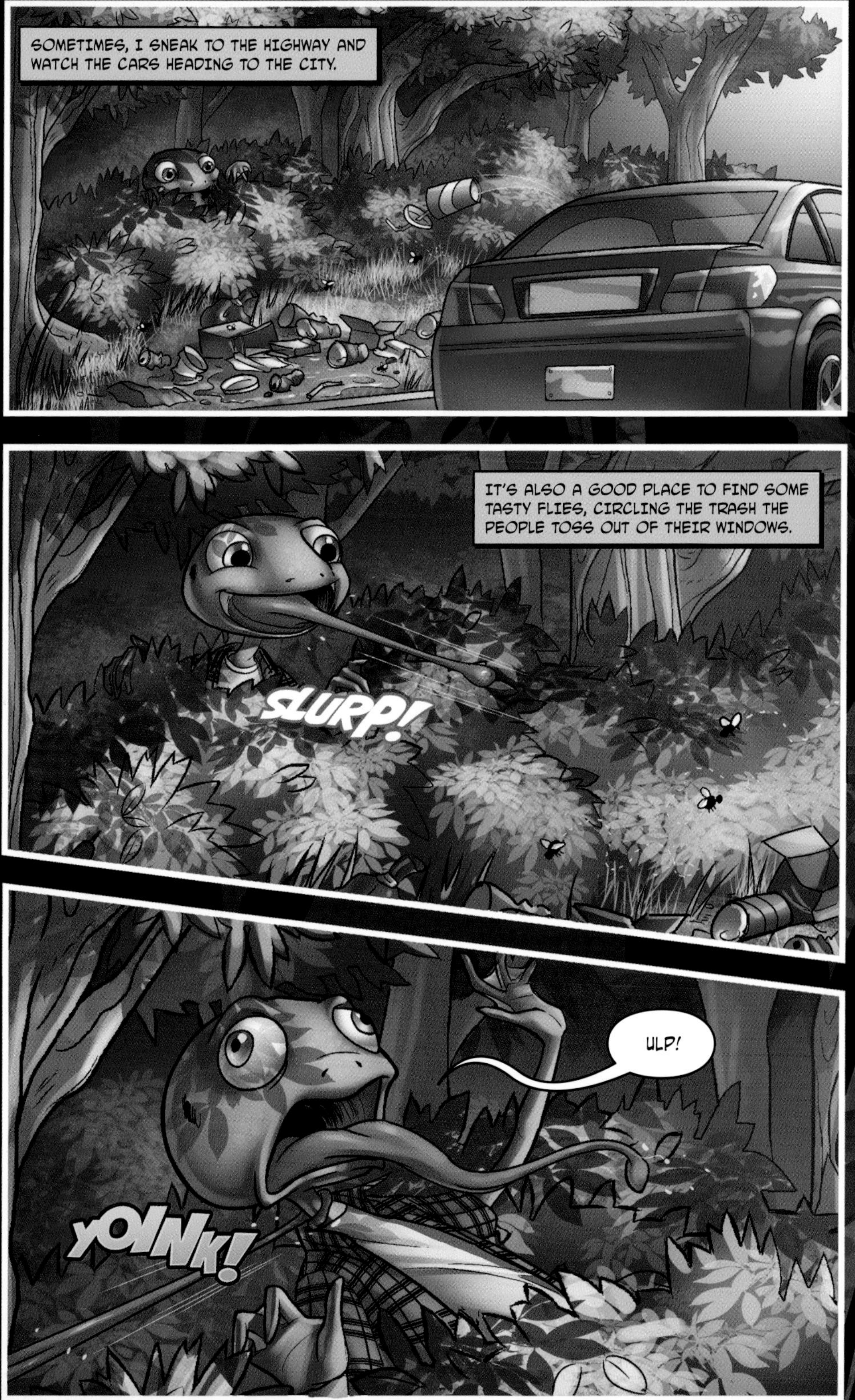
SOMETIMES, I SNEAK TO THE HIGHWAY AND WATCH THE CARS HEADING TO THE CITY.
IT'S ALSO A GOOD PLACE TO FIND SOME TASTY FLIES, CIRCLING THE TRASH THE PEOPLE TOSS OUT OF THEIR WINDOWS.
SLURP!
ULP!
YOINK!

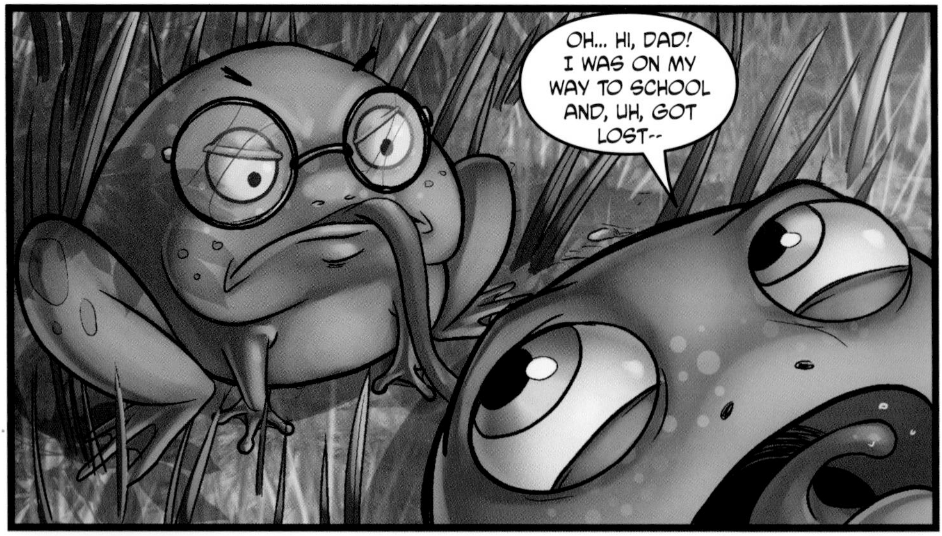
OH... HI, DAD! I WAS ON MY WAY TO SCHOOL AND, UH, GOT LOST--

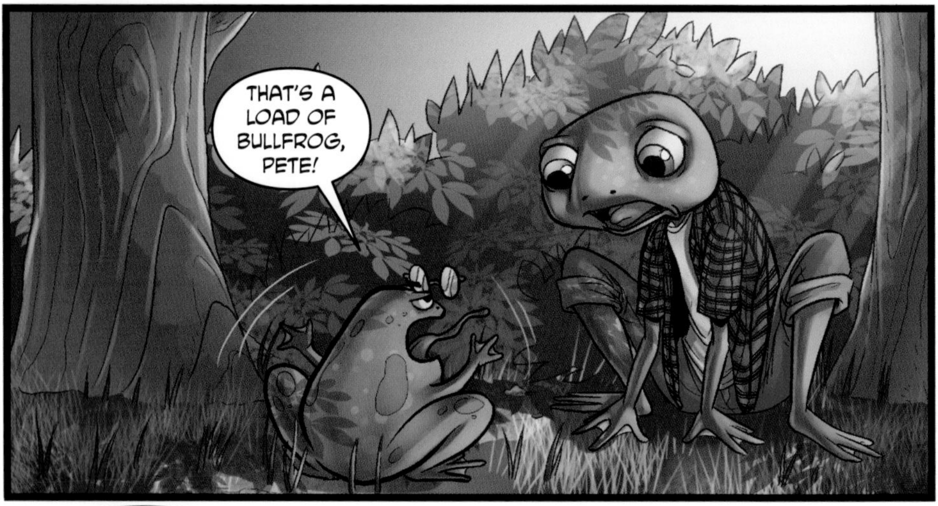
THAT'S A LOAD OF BULLFROG, PETE!

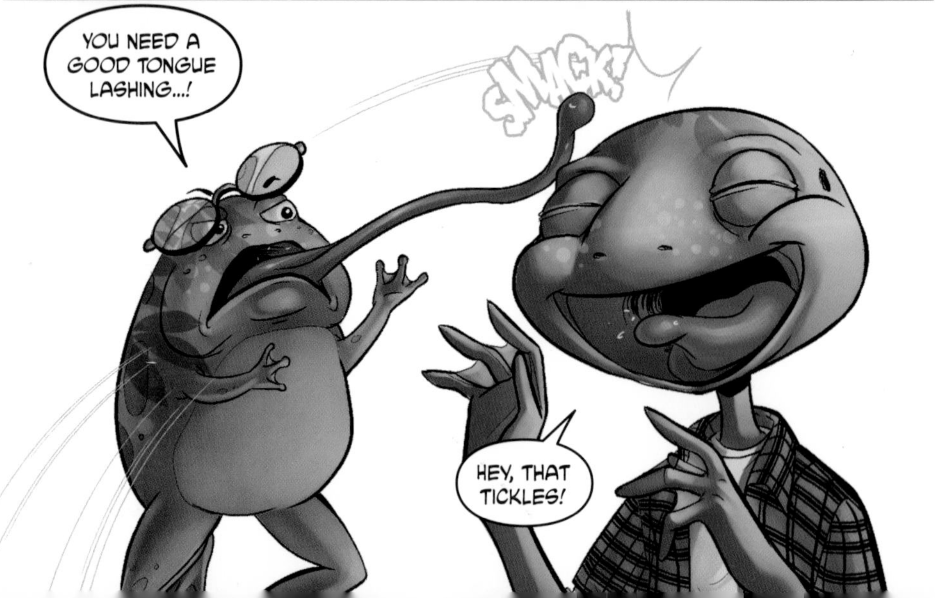
YOU NEED A GOOD TONGUE LASHING...!
SMACK!
HEY, THAT TICKLES!

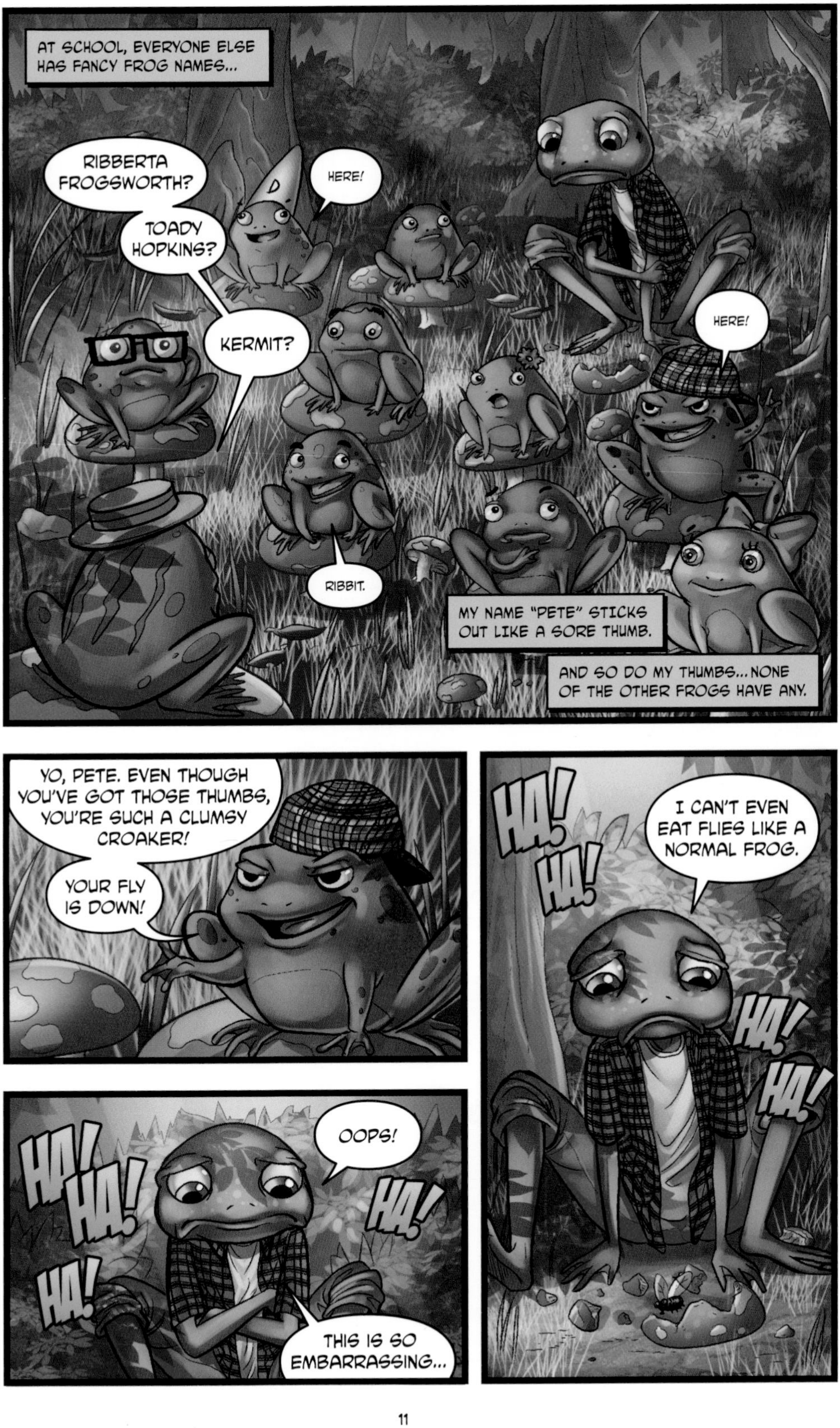
AT SCHOOL, EVERYONE ELSE HAS FANCY FROG NAMES...
RIBBERTA FROGSWORTH?
HERE!
TOADY HOPKINS?
KERMIT?
HERE!
RIBBIT.
MY NAME "PETE" STICKS OUT LIKE A SORE THUMB.
AND SO DO MY THUMBS... NONE OF THE OTHER FROGS HAVE ANY.
YO, PETE. EVEN THOUGH YOU'VE GOT THOSE THUMBS, YOU'RE SUCH A CLUMSY CROAKER!
YOUR FLY IS DOWN!
HA! HA! HA!
OOPS!
HA!
THIS IS SO EMBARRASSING...
HA! HA!
I CAN'T EVEN EAT FLIES LIKE A NORMAL FROG.
HA! HA!

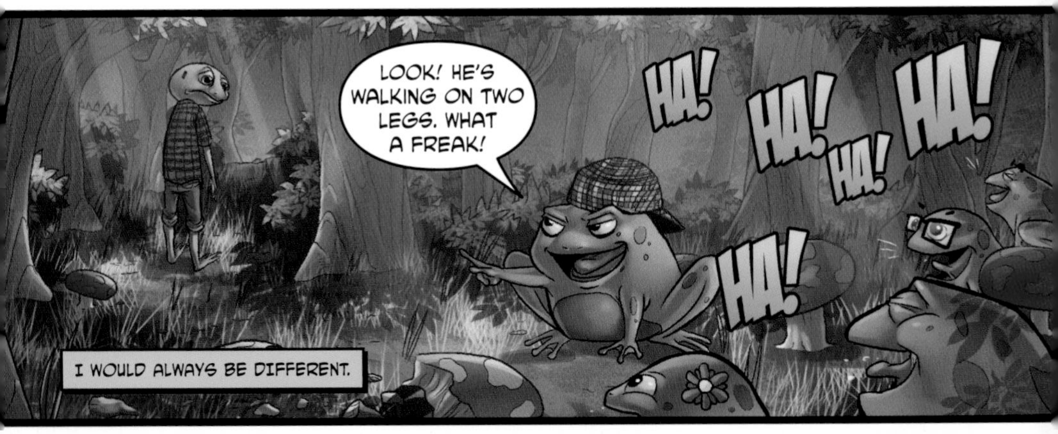
LOOK! HE'S WALKING ON TWO LEGS. WHAT A FREAK!
HA! HA! HA! HA! HA!
I WOULD ALWAYS BE DIFFERENT.

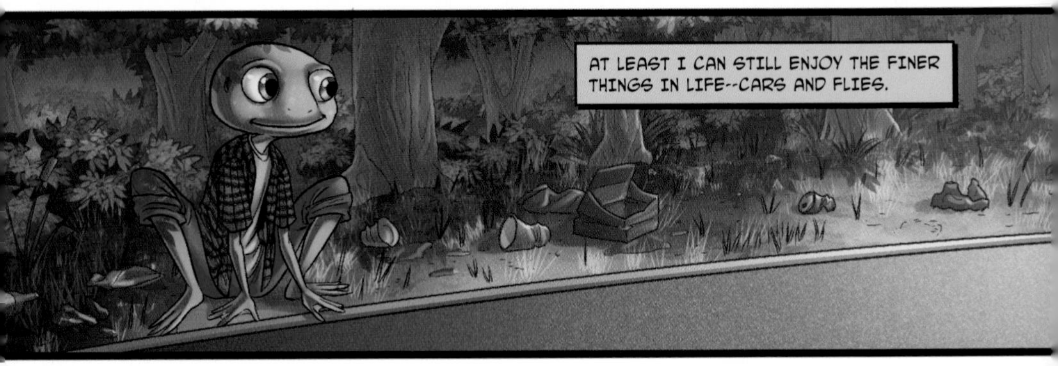
AT LEAST I CAN STILL ENJOY THE FINER THINGS IN LIFE--CARS AND FLIES.

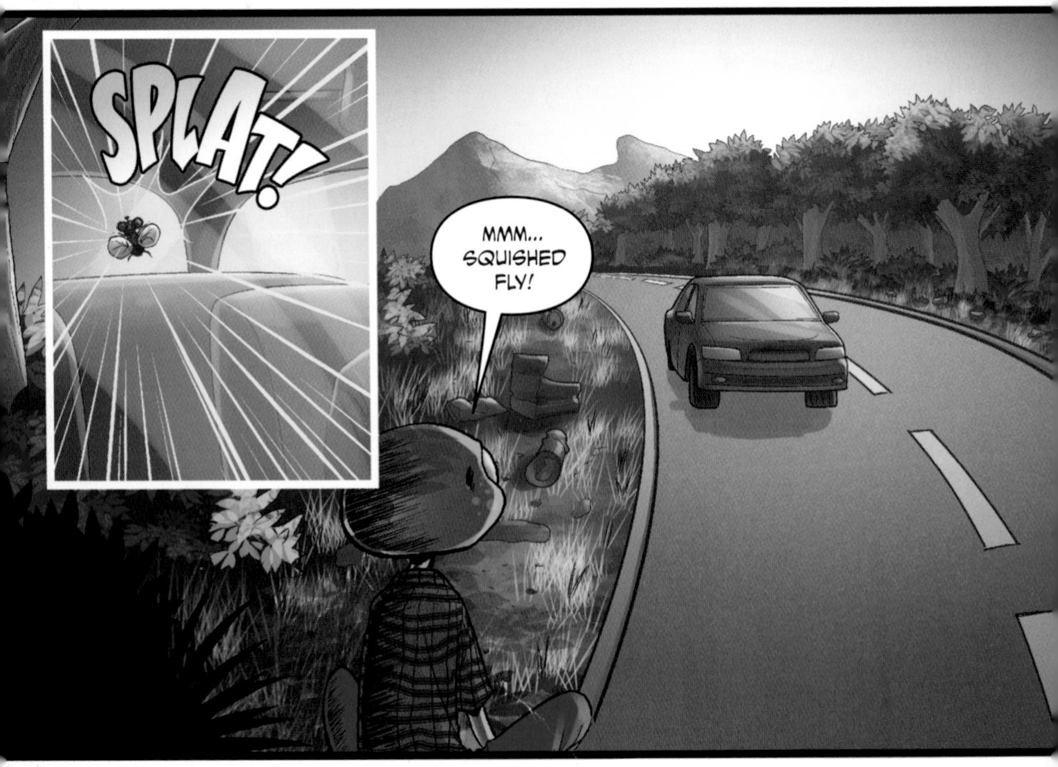
SPLAT!
MMM... SQUISHED FLY!

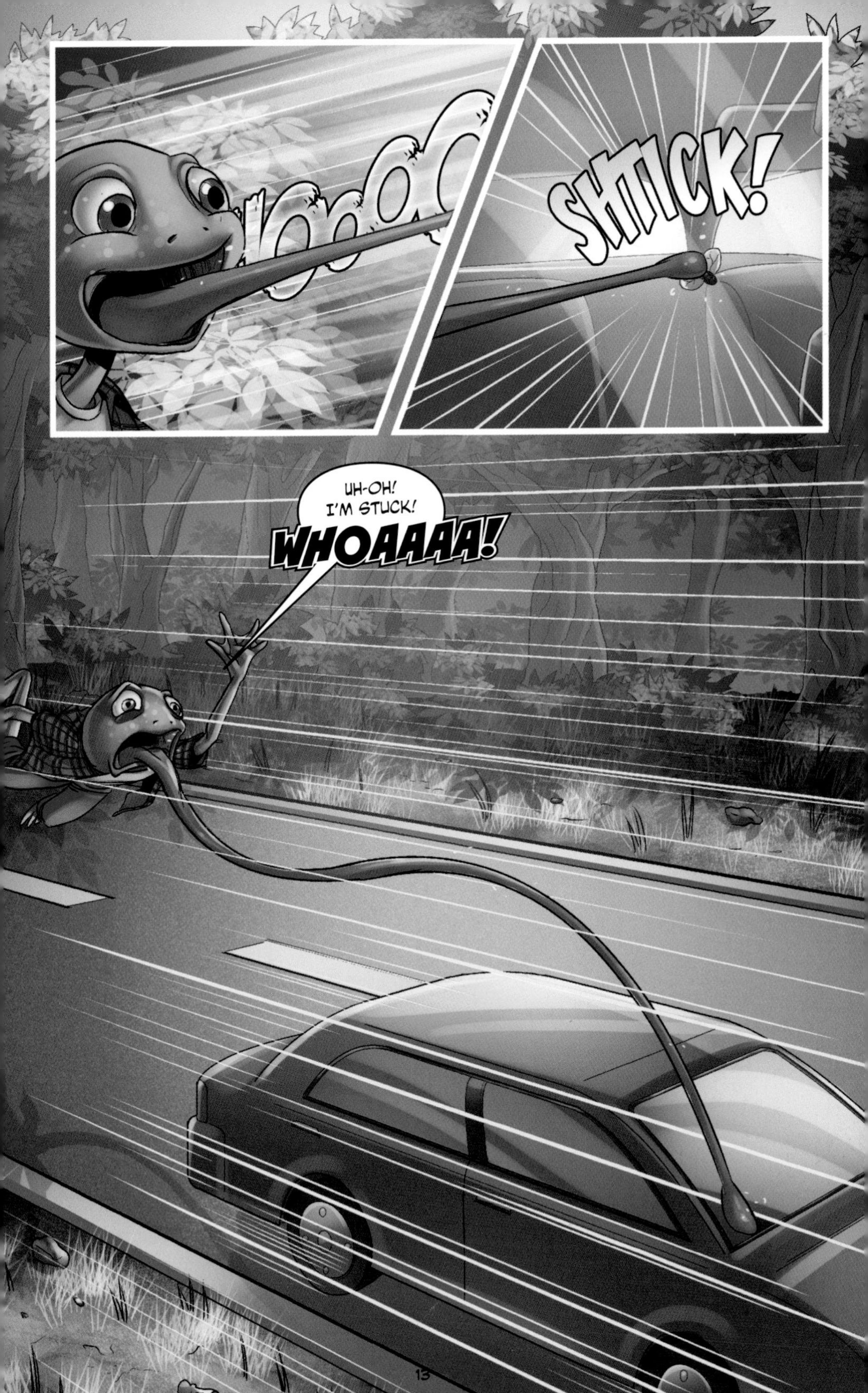
SHTICK!
UH-OH! I'M STUCK!
WHOAAAA!

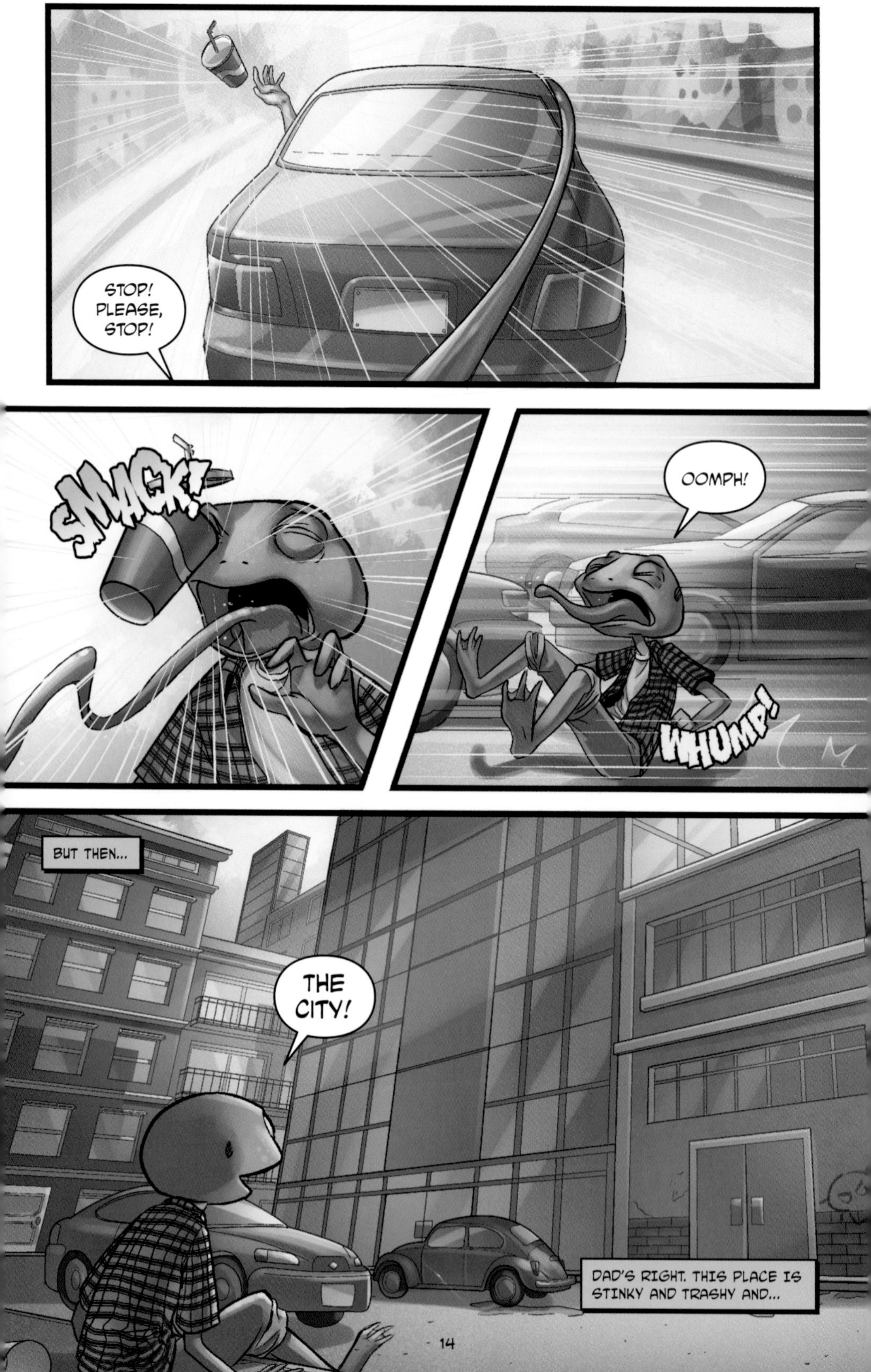
STOP! PLEASE, STOP!
SMACK!
OOMPH!
WHUMP!
BUT THEN...
THE CITY!
DAD'S RIGHT. THIS PLACE IS STINKY AND TRASHY AND...

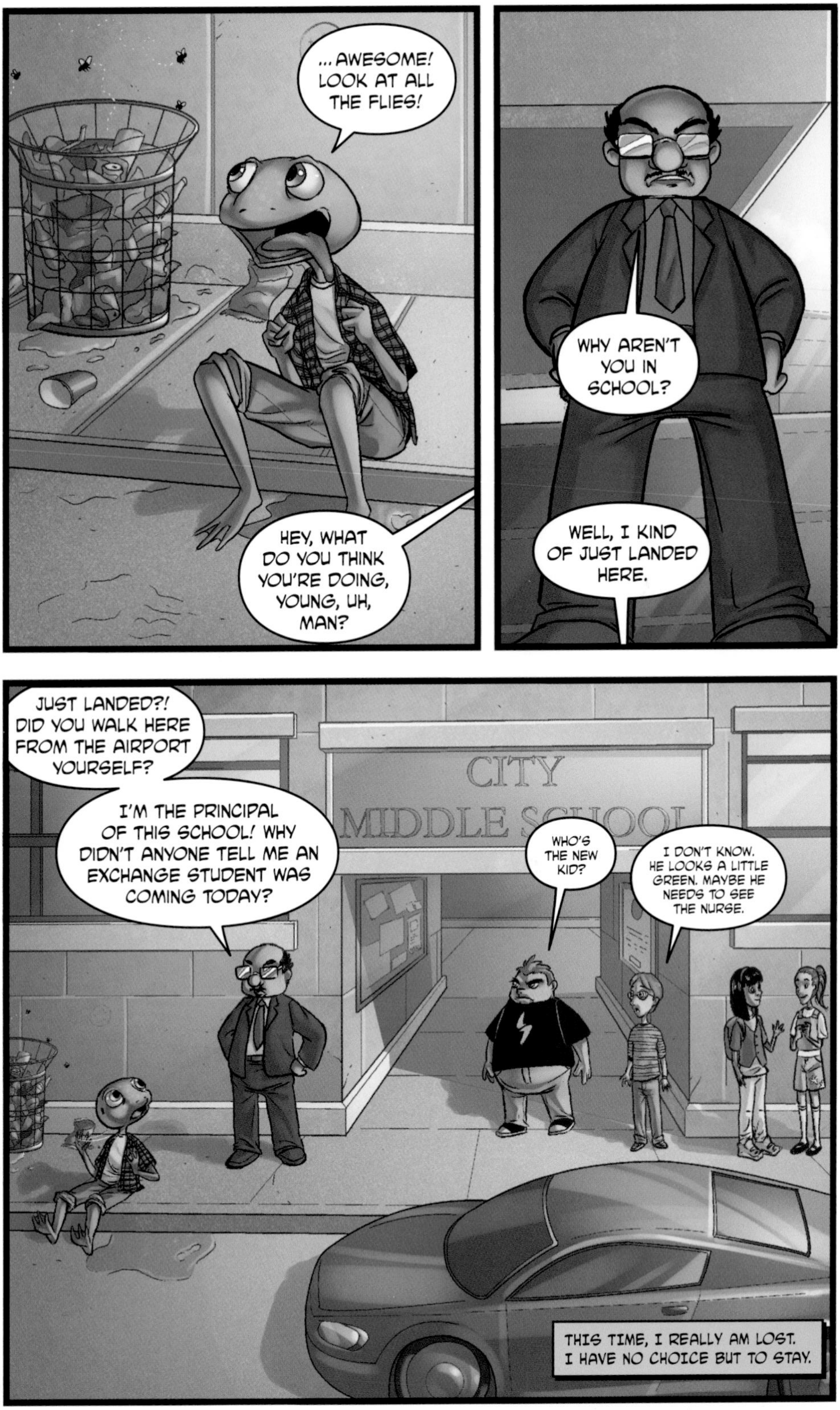
...AWESOME! LOOK AT ALL THE FLIES!
HEY, WHAT DO YOU THINK YOU'RE DOING, YOUNG, UH, MAN?
WHY AREN'T YOU IN SCHOOL?
WELL, I KIND OF JUST LANDED HERE.
JUST LANDED?! DID YOU WALK HERE FROM THE AIRPORT YOURSELF?
I'M THE PRINCIPAL OF THIS SCHOOL! WHY DIDN'T ANYONE TELL ME AN EXCHANGE STUDENT WAS COMING TODAY?
CITY
WHO'S THE NEW KID?
I DON'T KNOW. HE LOOKS A LITTLE GREEN. MAYBE HE NEEDS TO SEE THE NURSE.
THIS TIME, I REALLY AM LOST. I HAVE NO CHOICE BUT TO STAY.

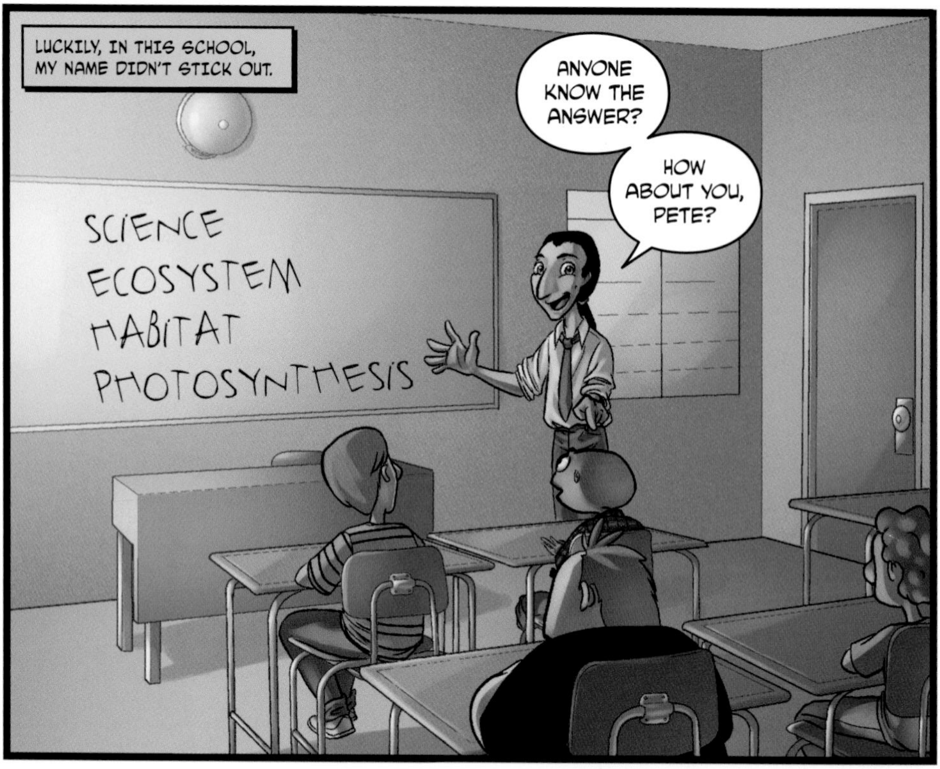
LUCKILY, IN THIS SCHOOL, MY NAME DIDN'T STICK OUT.
ANYONE KNOW THE ANSWER?
HOW ABOUT YOU, PETE?
SCIENCE
ECOSYSTEM
HABITAT
PHOTOSYNTHESIS

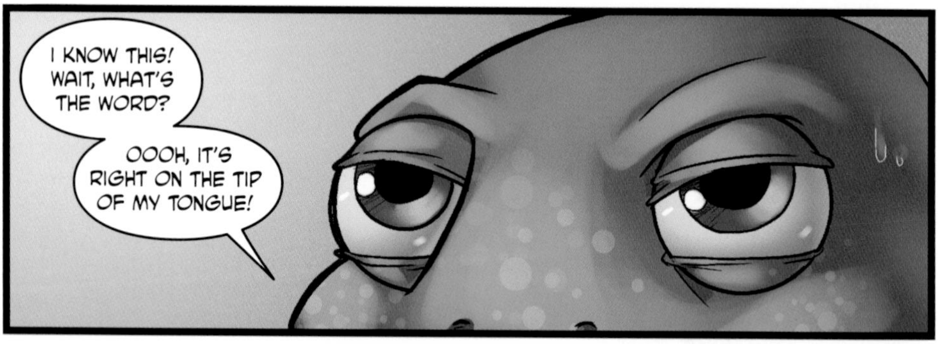
I KNOW THIS! WAIT, WHAT'S THE WORD?
OOOH, IT'S RIGHT ON THE TIP OF MY TONGUE!

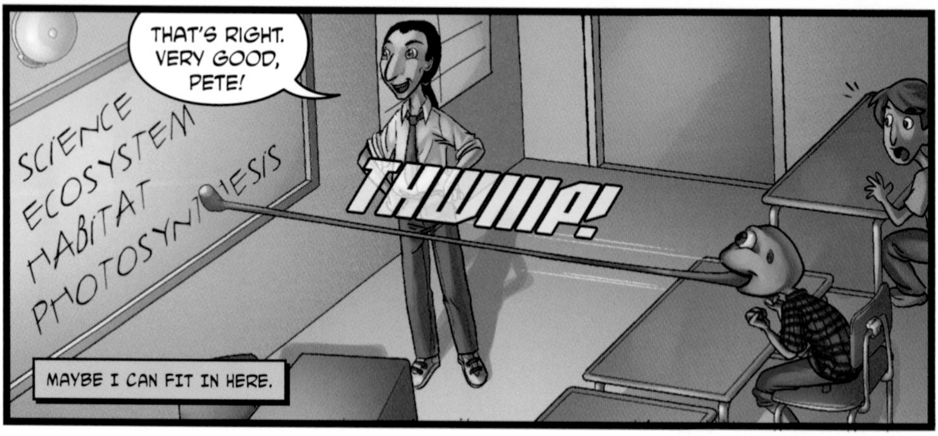
THAT'S RIGHT. VERY GOOD, PETE!
SCIENCE
ECOSYSTEM
HABITAT
PHOTOSYNTHESIS
THWIIIP!
MAYBE I CAN FIT IN HERE.

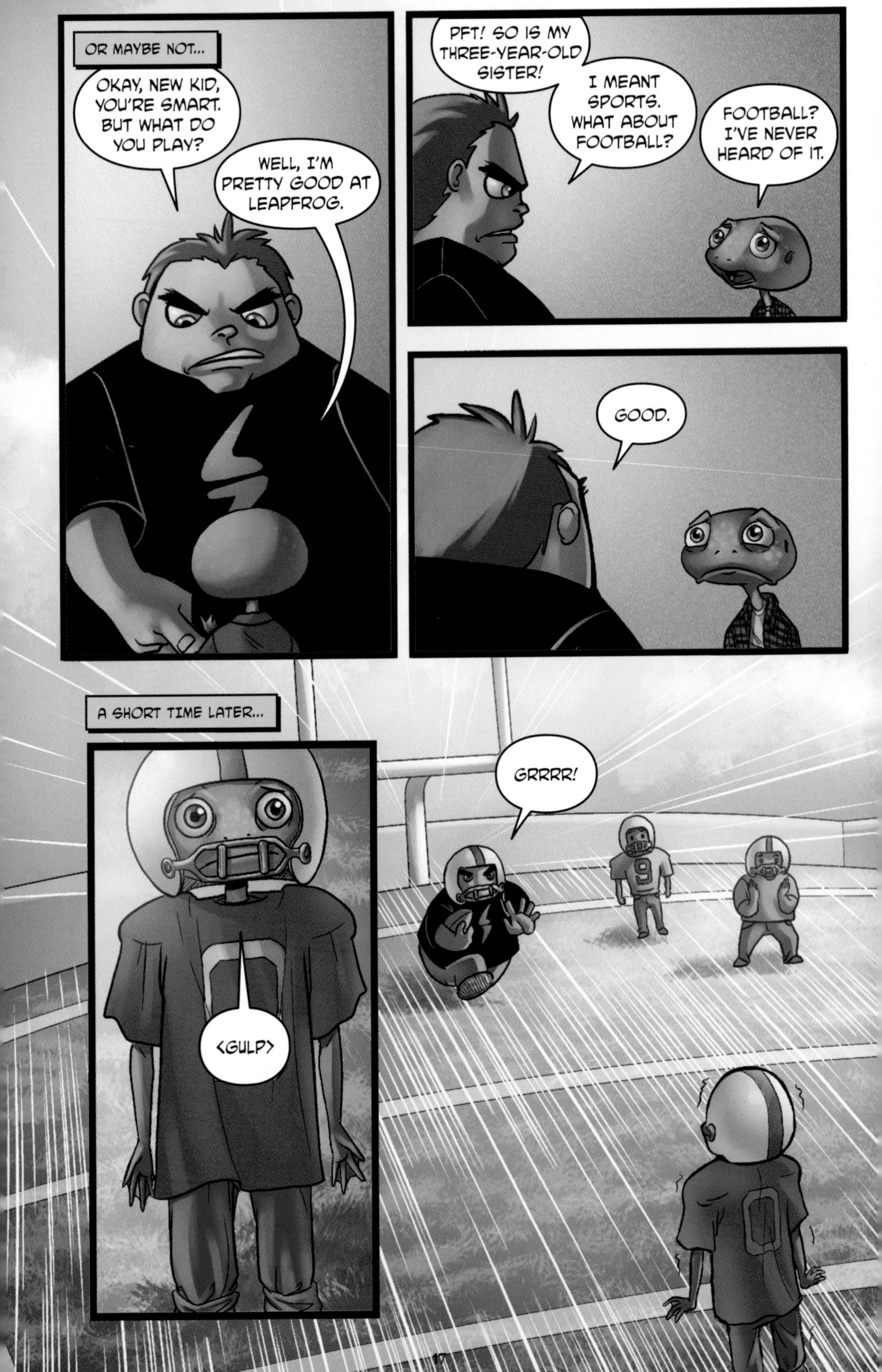
OR MAYBE NOT...
OKAY, NEW KID, YOU'RE SMART. BUT WHAT DO YOU PLAY?
WELL, I'M PRETTY GOOD AT LEAPFROG.
PFT! SO IS MY THREE-YEAR-OLD SISTER!
I MEANT SPORTS. WHAT ABOUT FOOTBALL?
FOOTBALL? I'VE NEVER HEARD OF IT.
GOOD.
A SHORT TIME LATER...
<GULP>
GRRRR!

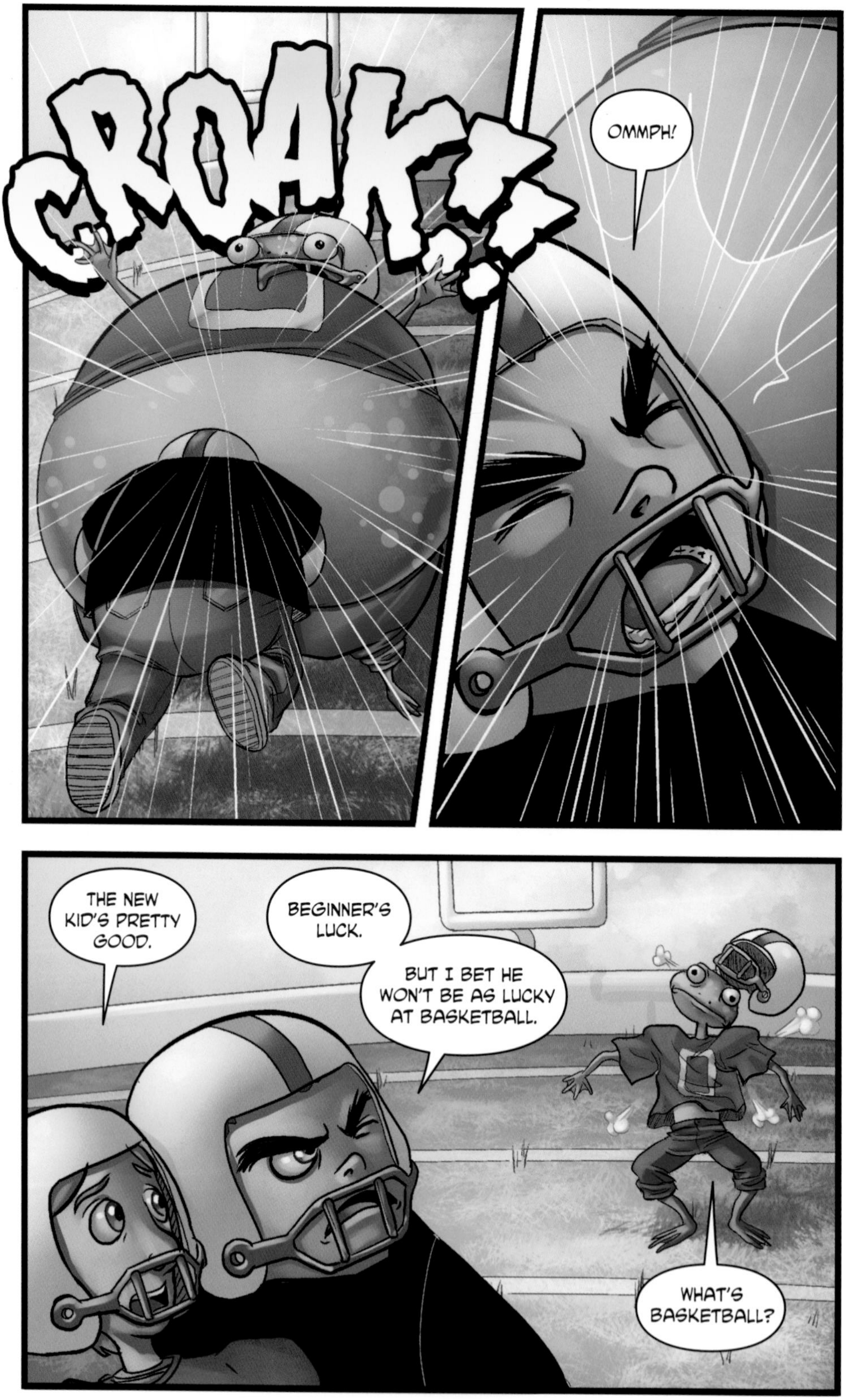
CROAK!
OMMPH!
THE NEW KID'S PRETTY GOOD.
BEGINNER'S LUCK.
BUT I BET HE WON'T BE AS LUCKY AT BASKETBALL.
WHAT'S BASKETBALL?

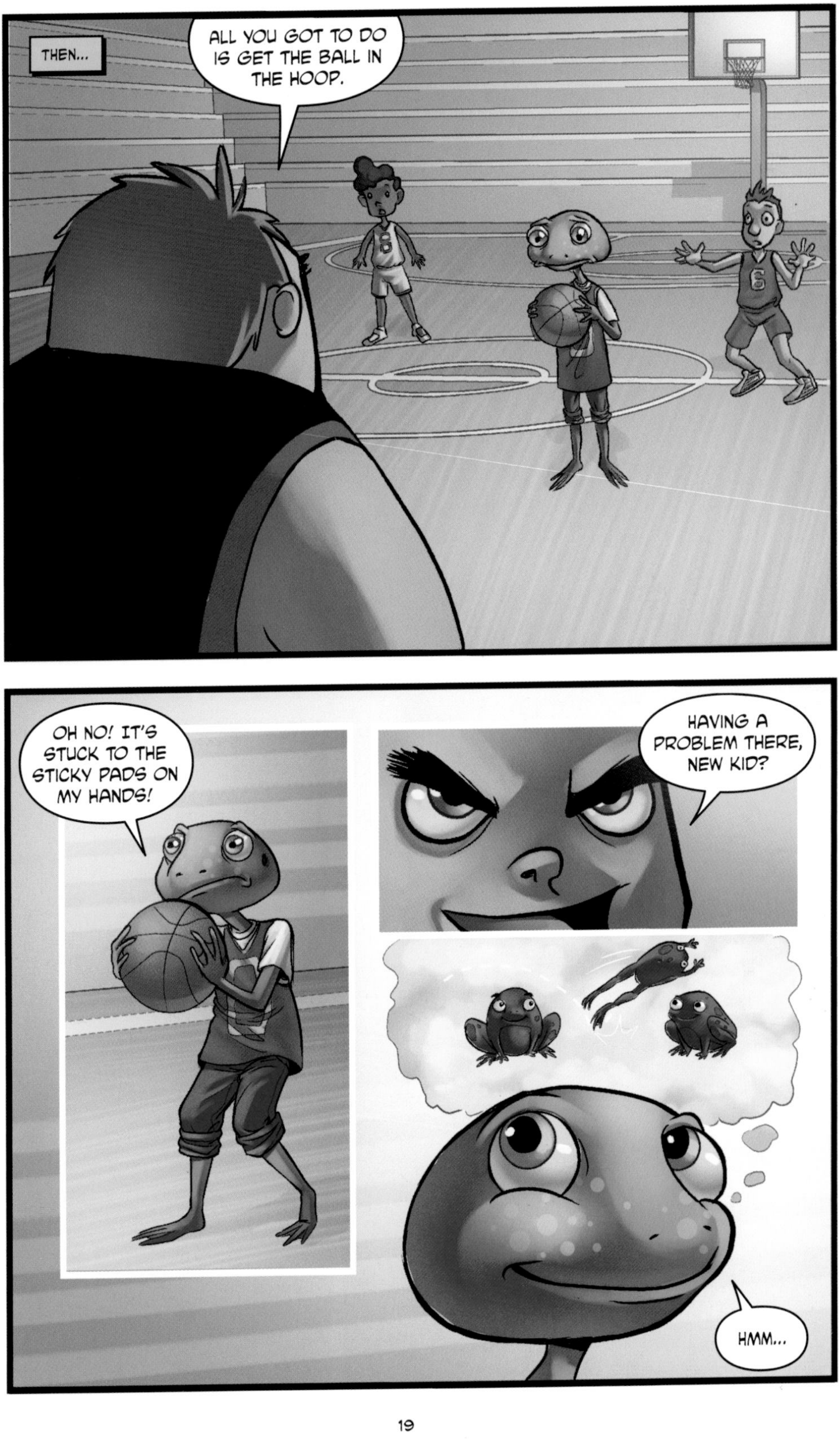
THEN...
ALL YOU GOT TO DO IS GET THE BALL IN THE HOOP.
OH NO! IT'S STUCK TO THE STICKY PADS ON MY HANDS!
HAVING A PROBLEM THERE, NEW KID?
HMM...

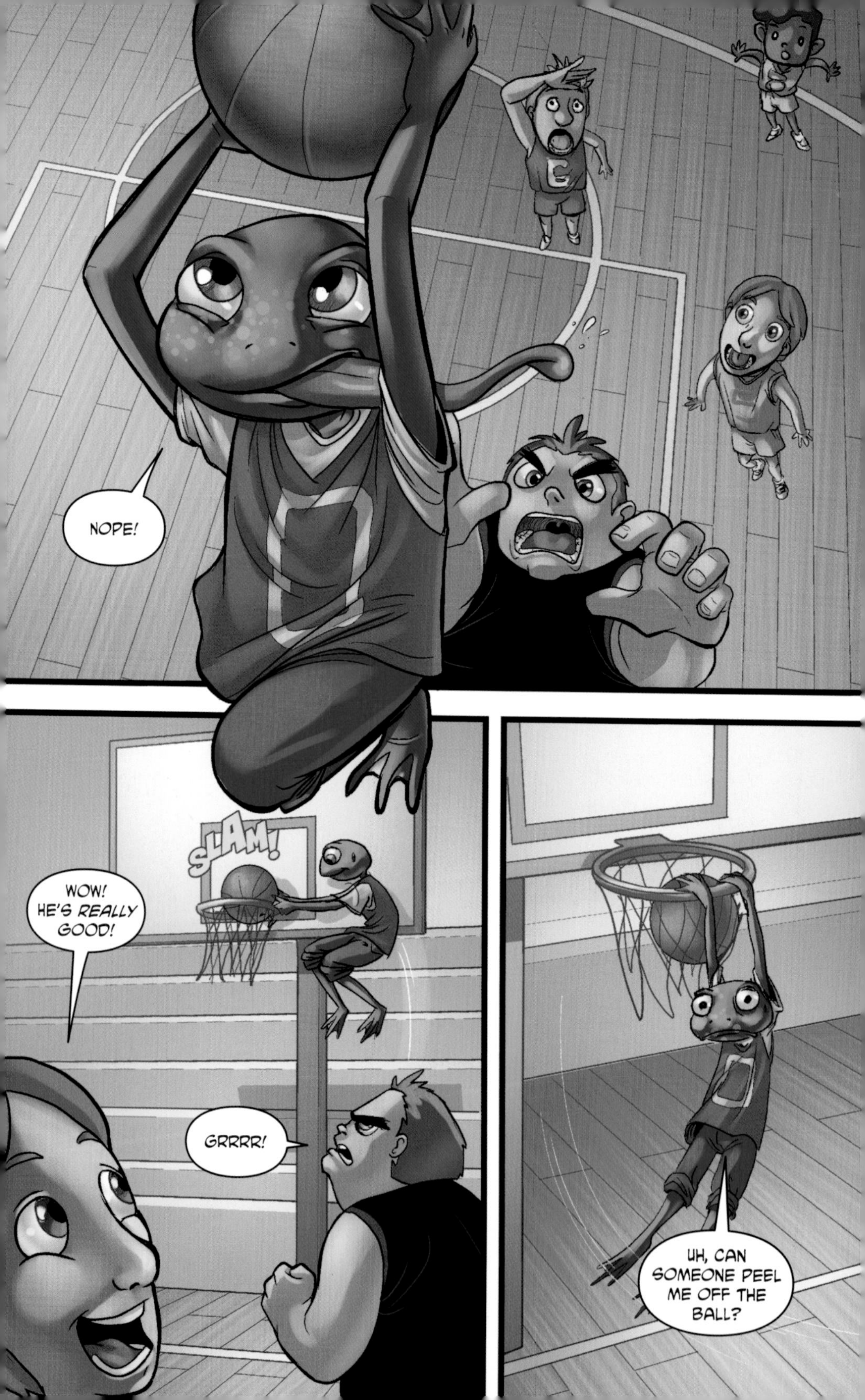
NOPE!
SLAM!
WOW! HE'S REALLY GOOD!
GRRRR!
UH, CAN SOMEONE PEEL ME OFF THE BALL?

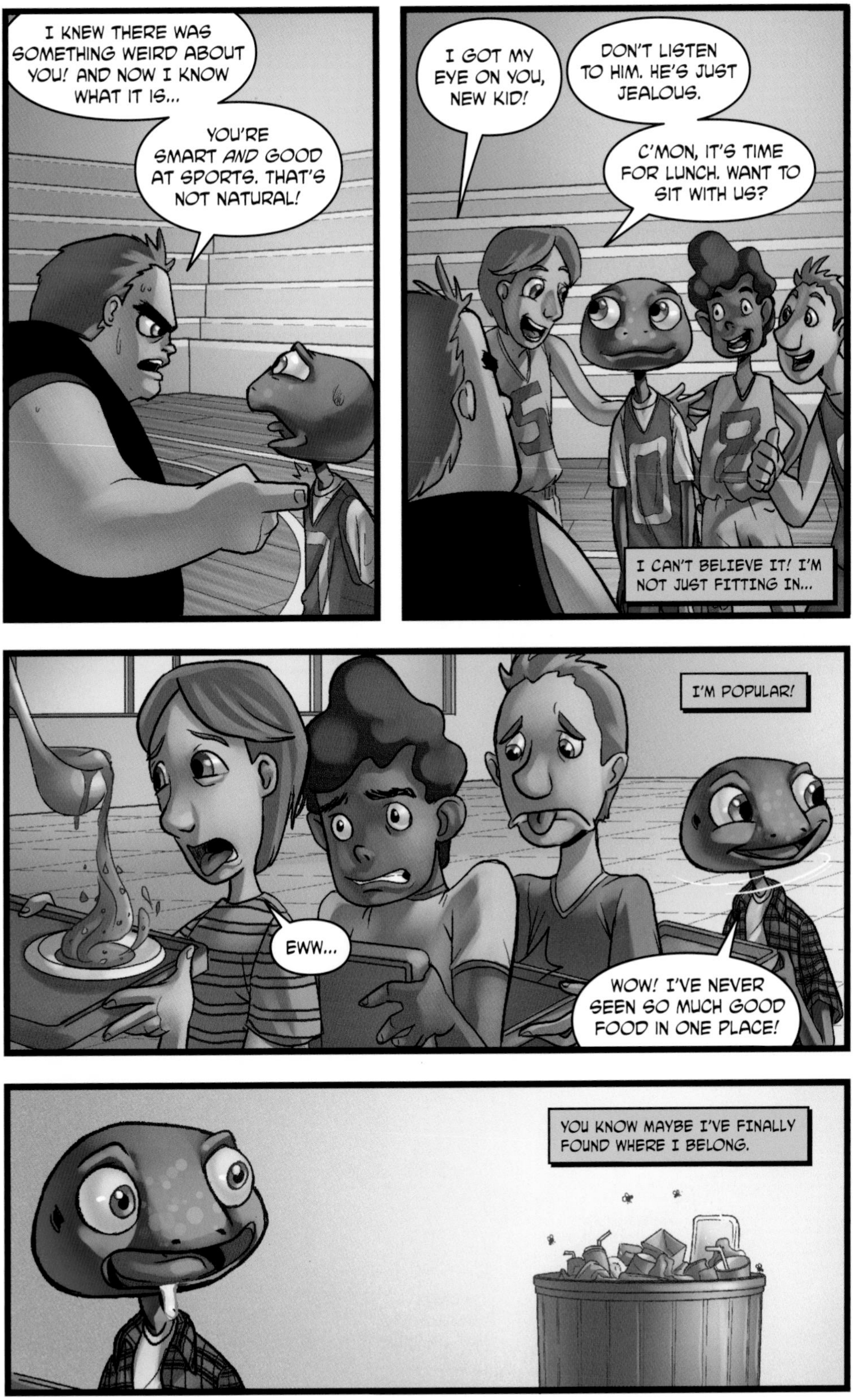
I KNEW THERE WAS SOMETHING WEIRD ABOUT YOU! AND NOW I KNOW WHAT IT IS...
YOU'RE SMART *AND* GOOD AT SPORTS. THAT'S NOT NATURAL!
I GOT MY EYE ON YOU, NEW KID!
DON'T LISTEN TO HIM. HE'S JUST JEALOUS.
C'MON, IT'S TIME FOR LUNCH. WANT TO SIT WITH US?
I CAN'T BELIEVE IT! I'M NOT JUST FITTING IN...
I'M POPULAR!
EWW...
WOW! I'VE NEVER SEEN SO MUCH GOOD FOOD IN ONE PLACE!
YOU KNOW MAYBE I'VE FINALLY FOUND WHERE I BELONG.

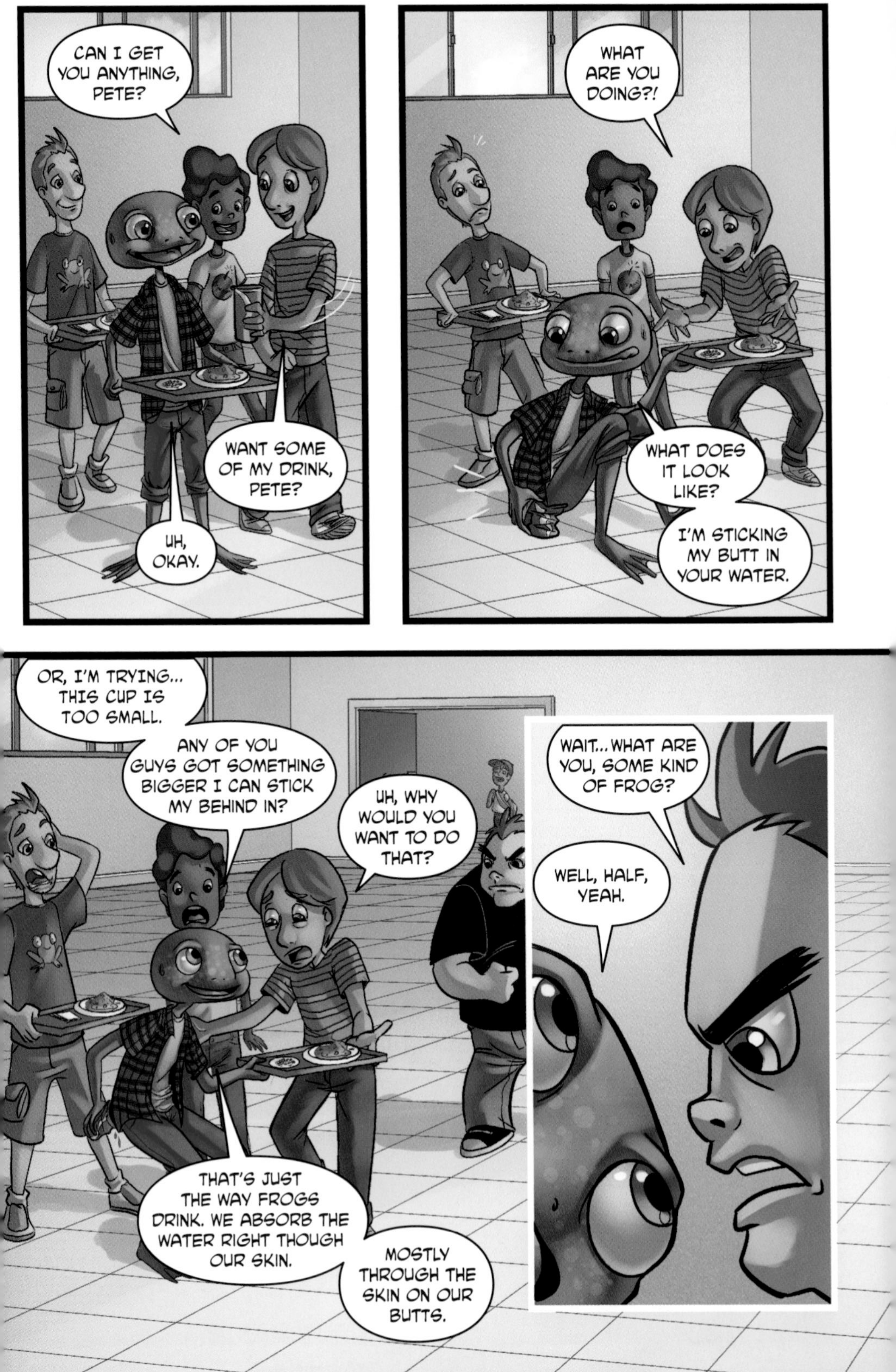
CAN I GET YOU ANYTHING, PETE?
WANT SOME OF MY DRINK, PETE?
UH, OKAY.
WHAT ARE YOU DOING?!
WHAT DOES IT LOOK LIKE?
I'M STICKING MY BUTT IN YOUR WATER.
OR, I'M TRYING... THIS CUP IS TOO SMALL.
ANY OF YOU GUYS GOT SOMETHING BIGGER I CAN STICK MY BEHIND IN?
UH, WHY WOULD YOU WANT TO DO THAT?
THAT'S JUST THE WAY FROGS DRINK. WE ABSORB THE WATER RIGHT THOUGH OUR SKIN.
MOSTLY THROUGH THE SKIN ON OUR BUTTS.
WAIT...WHAT ARE YOU, SOME KIND OF FROG?
WELL, HALF, YEAH.

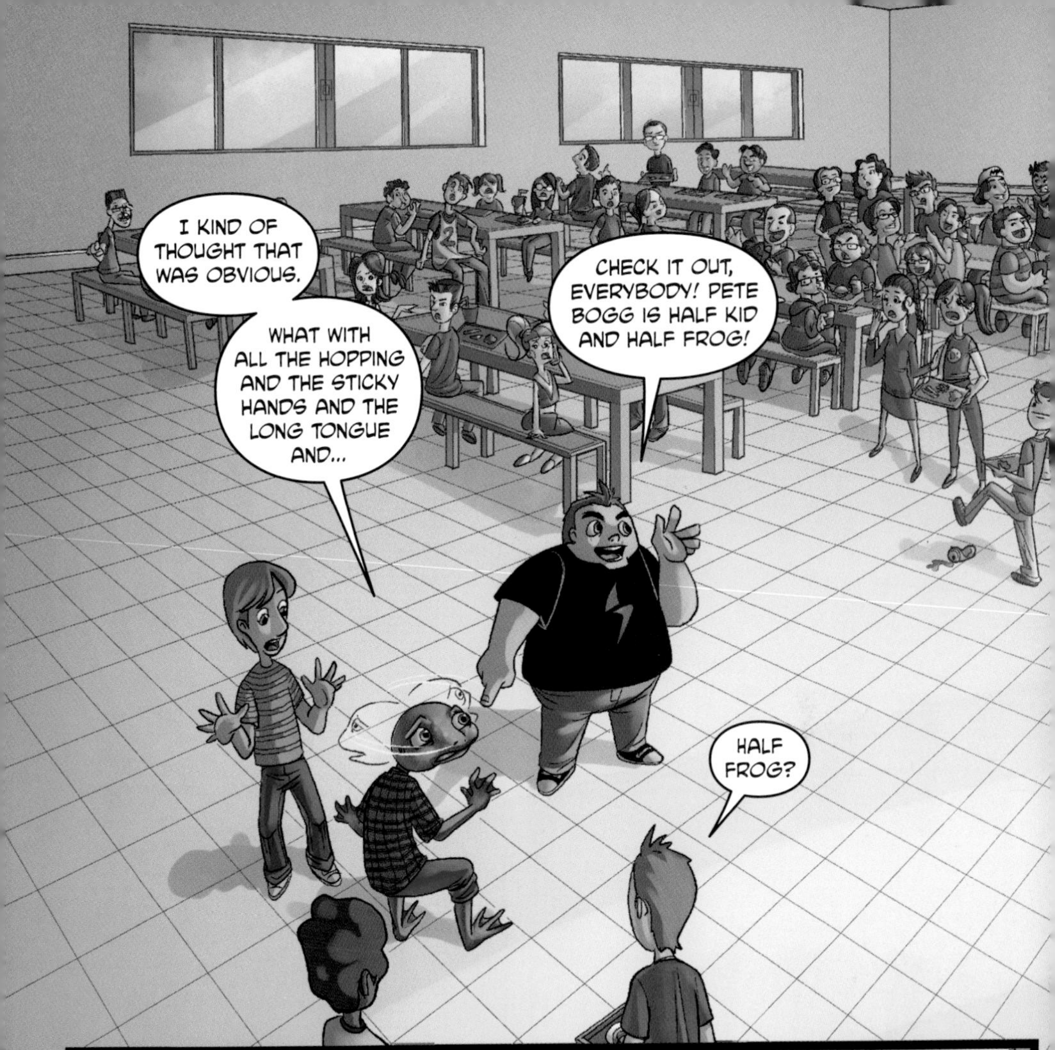
I KIND OF THOUGHT THAT WAS OBVIOUS.
WHAT WITH ALL THE HOPPING AND THE STICKY HANDS AND THE LONG TONGUE AND...
CHECK IT OUT, EVERYBODY! PETE BOGG IS HALF KID AND HALF FROG!
HALF FROG?

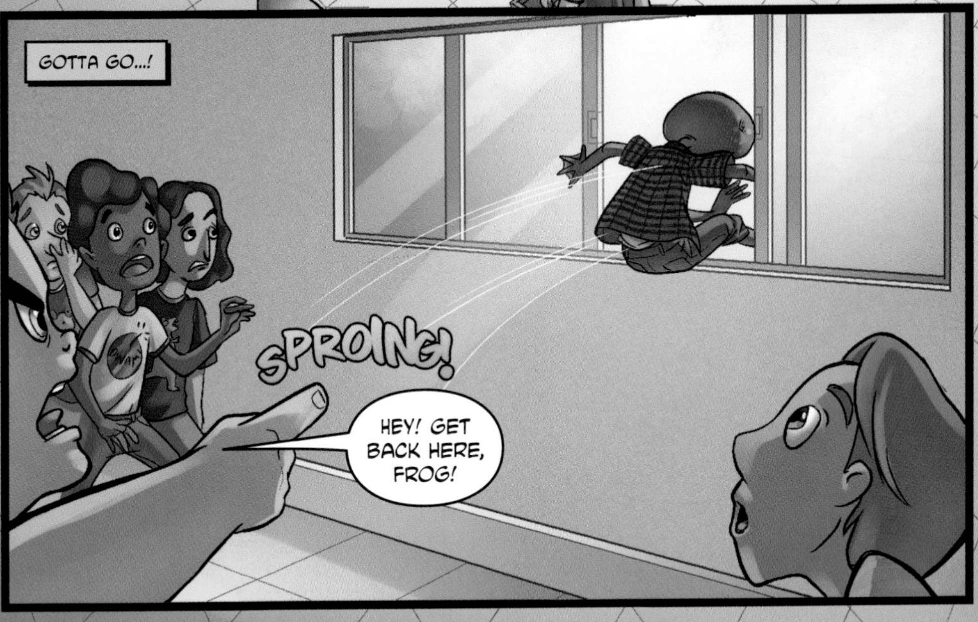
GOTTA GO...!
SPROING!
HEY! GET BACK HERE, FROG!

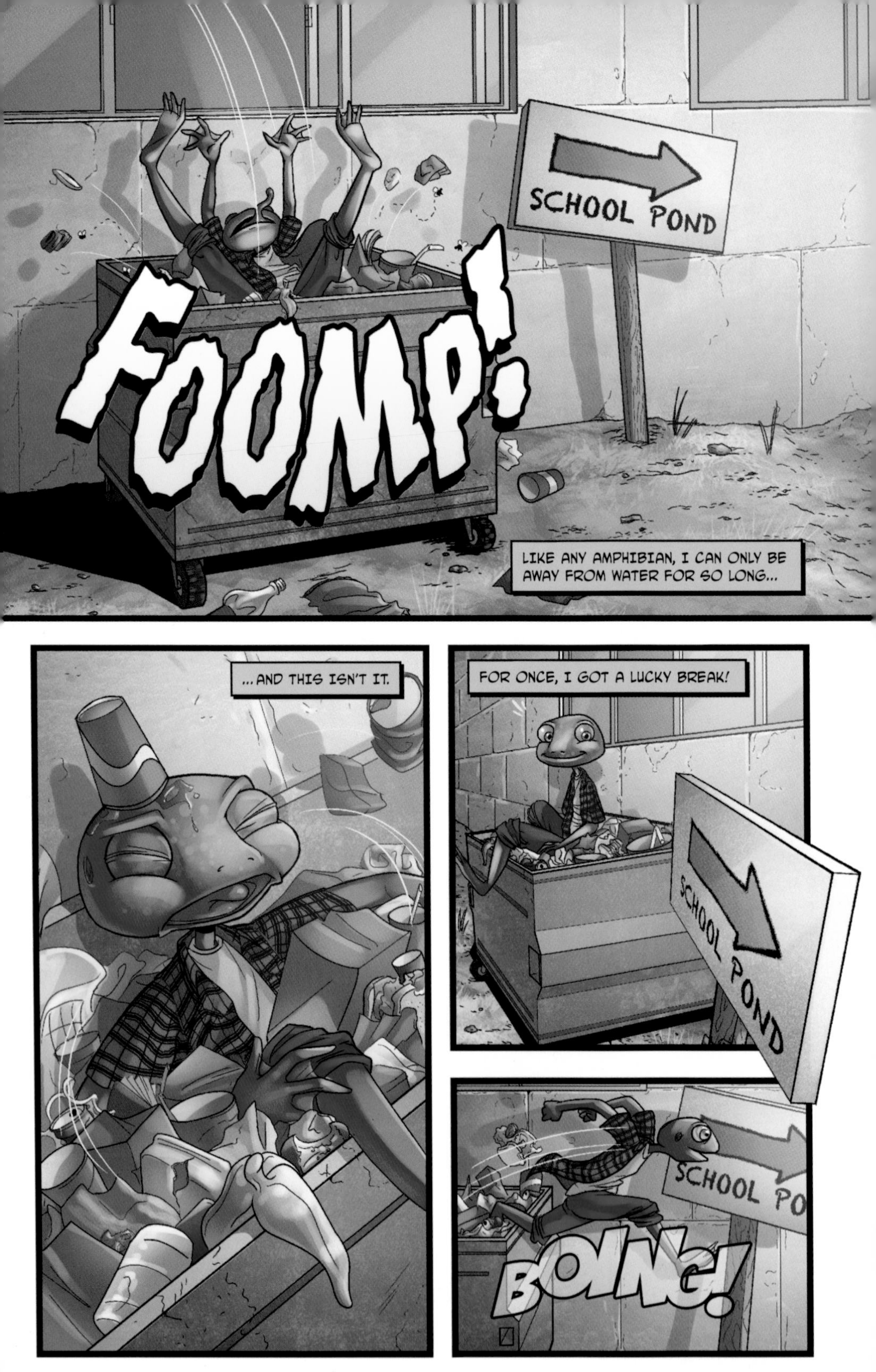
SCHOOL POND
FOOMP!
LIKE ANY AMPHIBIAN, I CAN ONLY BE AWAY FROM WATER FOR SO LONG...
...AND THIS ISN'T IT.
FOR ONCE, I GOT A LUCKY BREAK!
SCHOOL POND
SCHOOL PO
BOING!

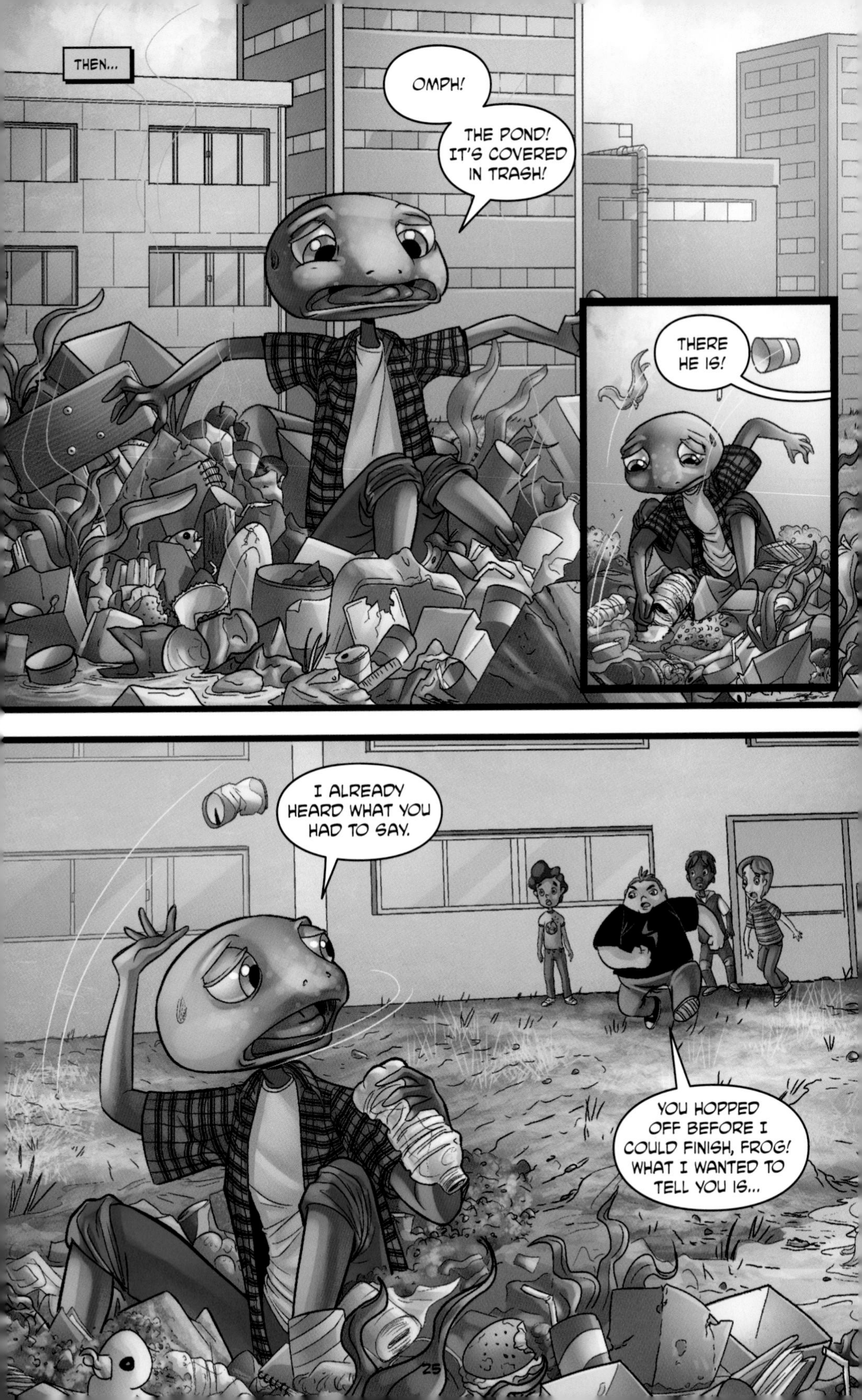
THEN...
OMPH!
THE POND! IT'S COVERED IN TRASH!
THERE HE IS!
I ALREADY HEARD WHAT YOU HAD TO SAY.
YOU HOPPED OFF BEFORE I COULD FINISH, FROG! WHAT I WANTED TO TELL YOU IS...

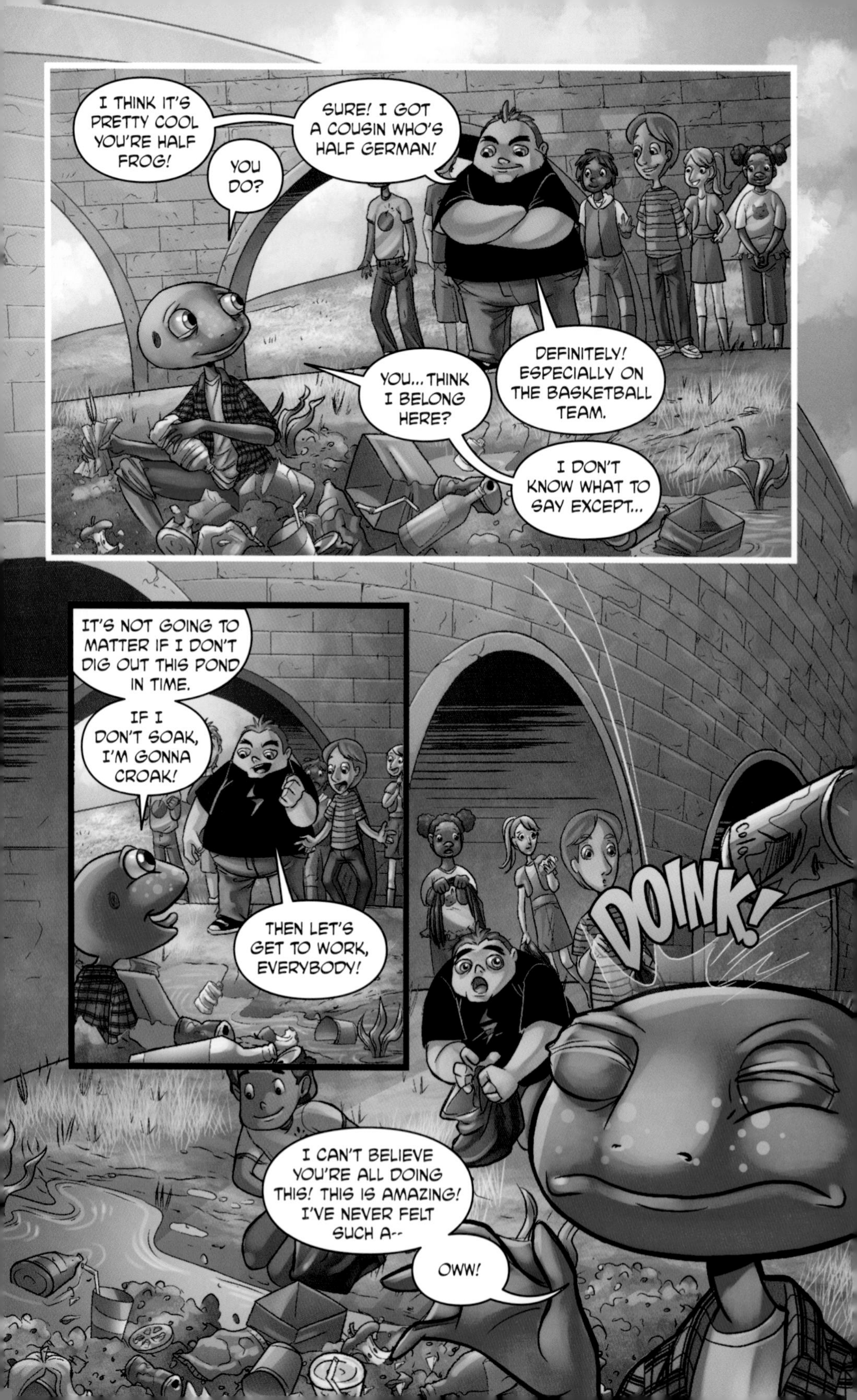
I THINK IT'S PRETTY COOL YOU'RE HALF FROG!
YOU DO?
SURE! I GOT A COUSIN WHO'S HALF GERMAN!
YOU...THINK I BELONG HERE?
DEFINITELY! ESPECIALLY ON THE BASKETBALL TEAM.
I DON'T KNOW WHAT TO SAY EXCEPT...
IT'S NOT GOING TO MATTER IF I DON'T DIG OUT THIS POND IN TIME.
IF I DON'T SOAK, I'M GONNA CROAK!
THEN LET'S GET TO WORK, EVERYBODY!
DOINK!
I CAN'T BELIEVE YOU'RE ALL DOING THIS! THIS IS AMAZING! I'VE NEVER FELT SUCH A--
OWW!

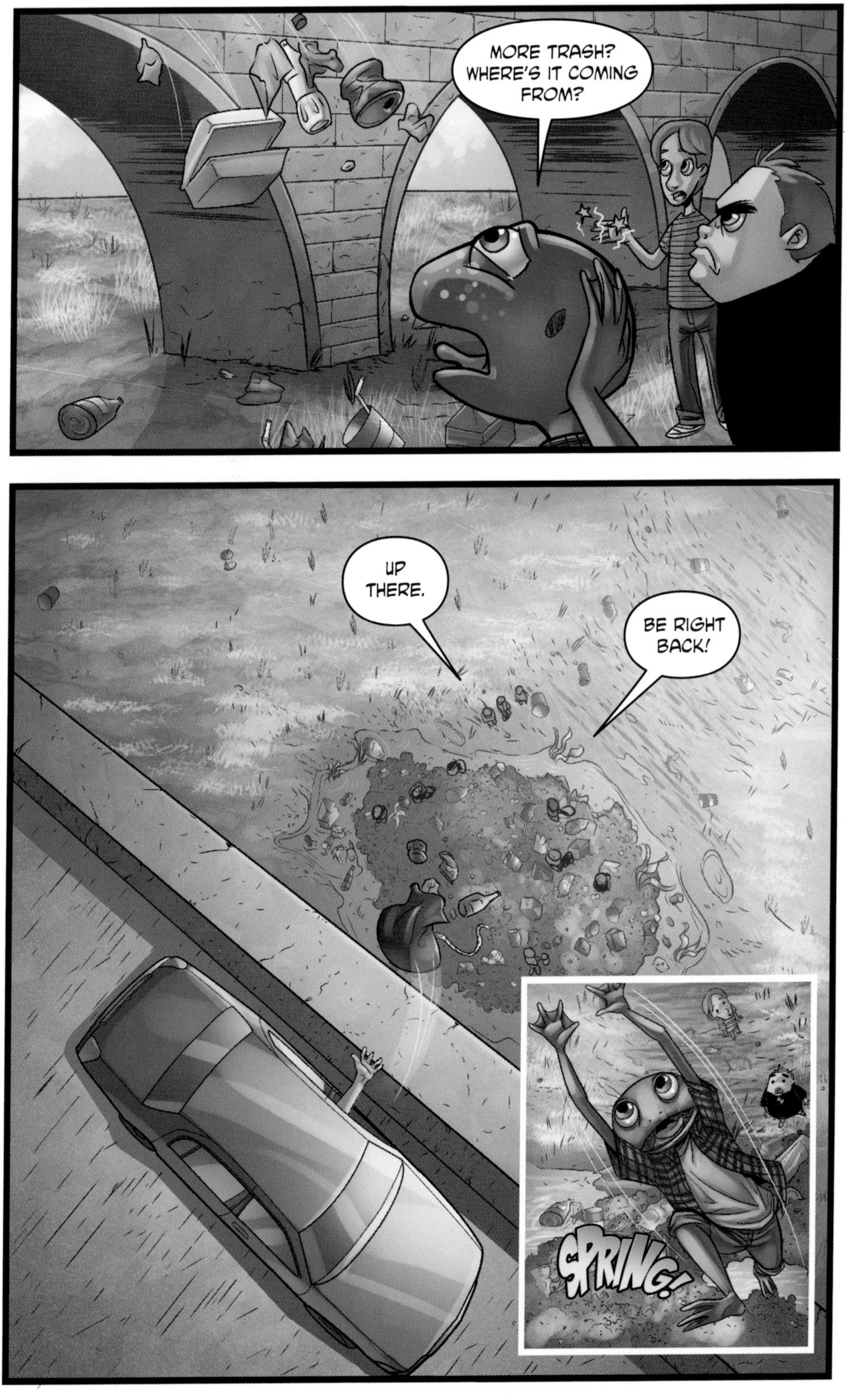
MORE TRASH? WHERE'S IT COMING FROM?
UP THERE.
BE RIGHT BACK!
SPRING!

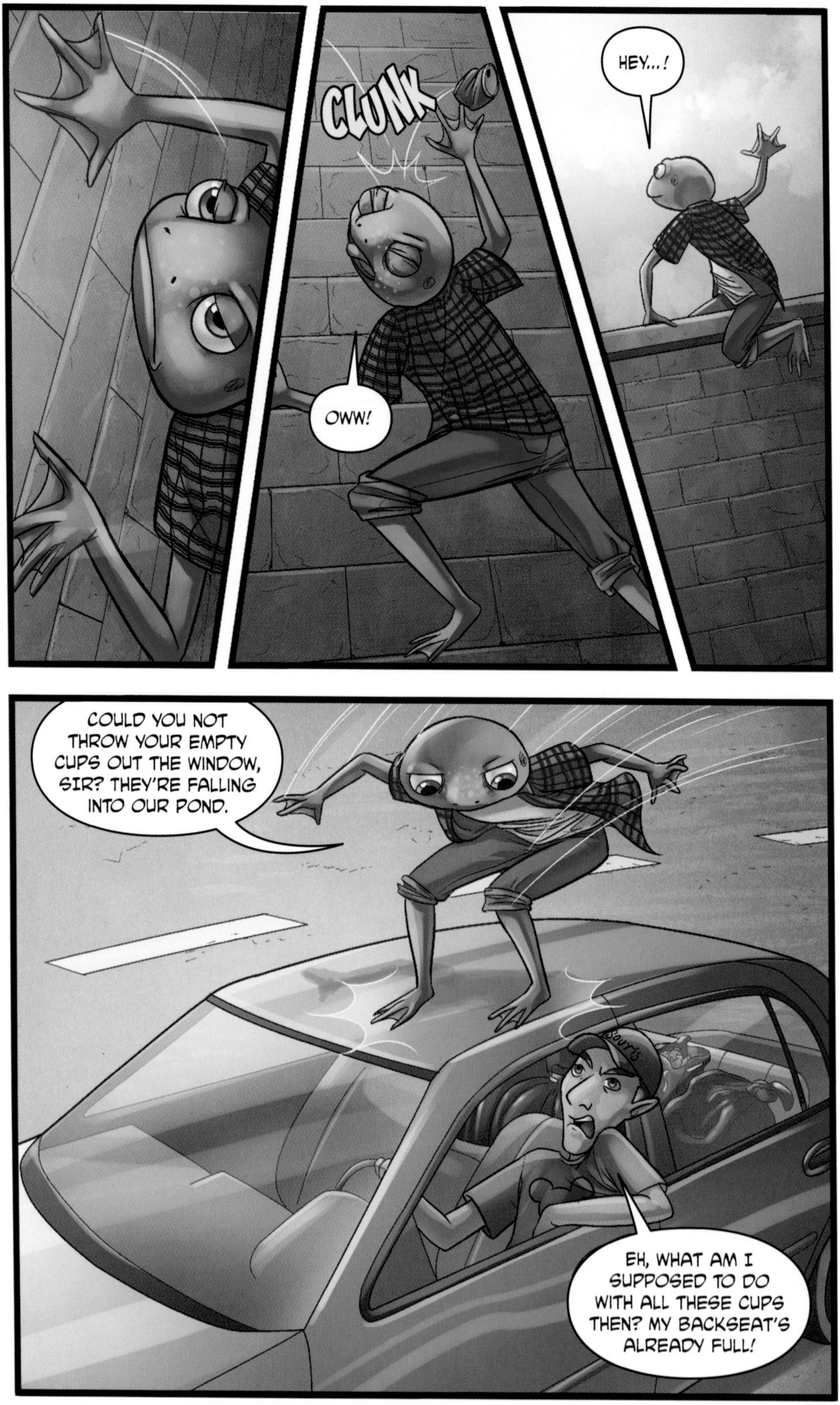
CLUNK
OWW!
HEY...!
COULD YOU NOT THROW YOUR EMPTY CUPS OUT THE WINDOW, SIR? THEY'RE FALLING INTO OUR POND.
EH, WHAT AM I SUPPOSED TO DO WITH ALL THESE CUPS THEN? MY BACKSEAT'S ALREADY FULL!

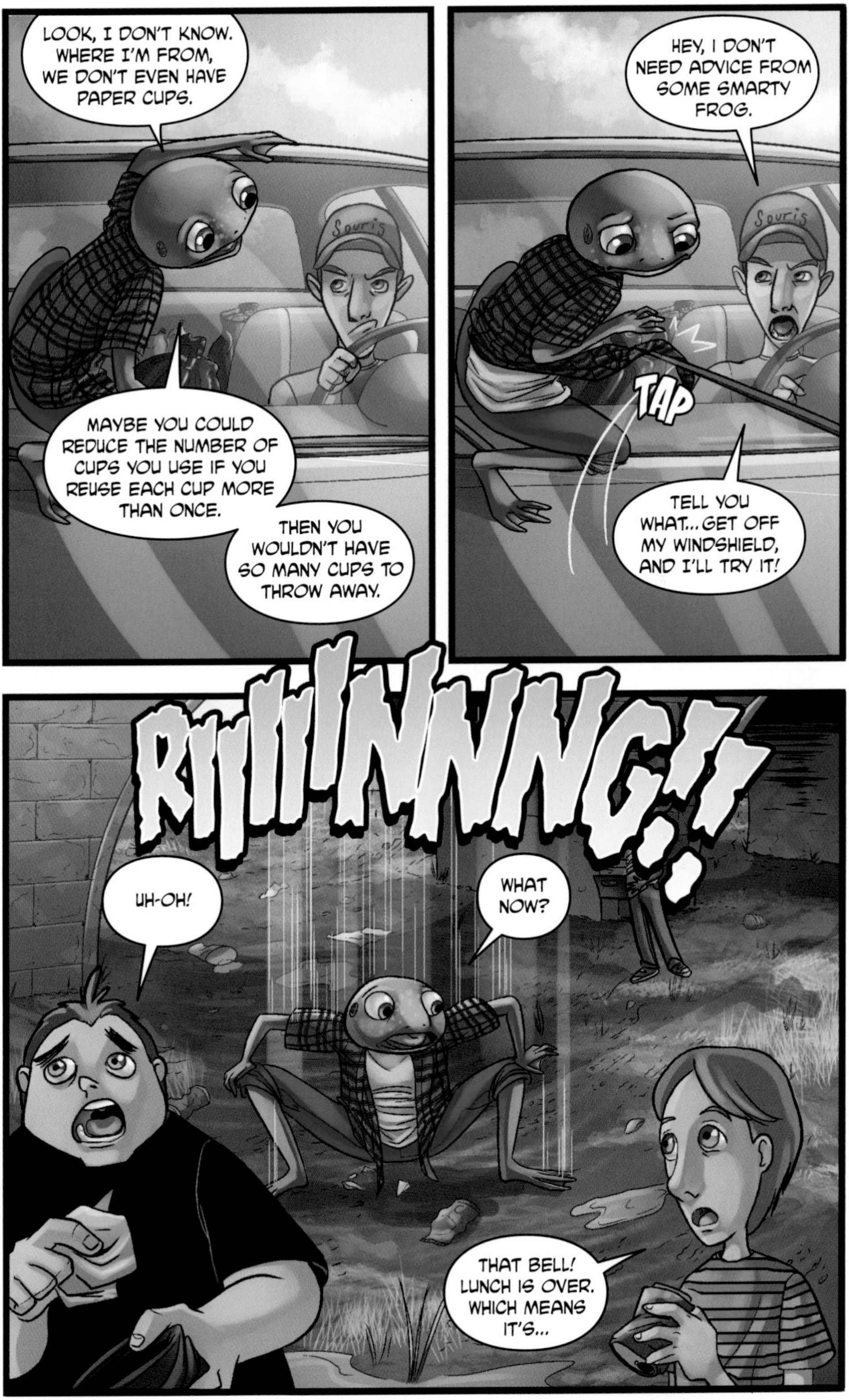
LOOK, I DON'T KNOW. WHERE I'M FROM, WE DON'T EVEN HAVE PAPER CUPS.
MAYBE YOU COULD REDUCE THE NUMBER OF CUPS YOU USE IF YOU REUSE EACH CUP MORE THAN ONCE.
THEN YOU WOULDN'T HAVE SO MANY CUPS TO THROW AWAY.
HEY, I DON'T NEED ADVICE FROM SOME SMARTY FROG.
TAP
TELL YOU WHAT...GET OFF MY WINDSHIELD, AND I'LL TRY IT!
RIIIINNNG!!
UH-OH!
WHAT NOW?
THAT BELL! LUNCH IS OVER. WHICH MEANS IT'S...

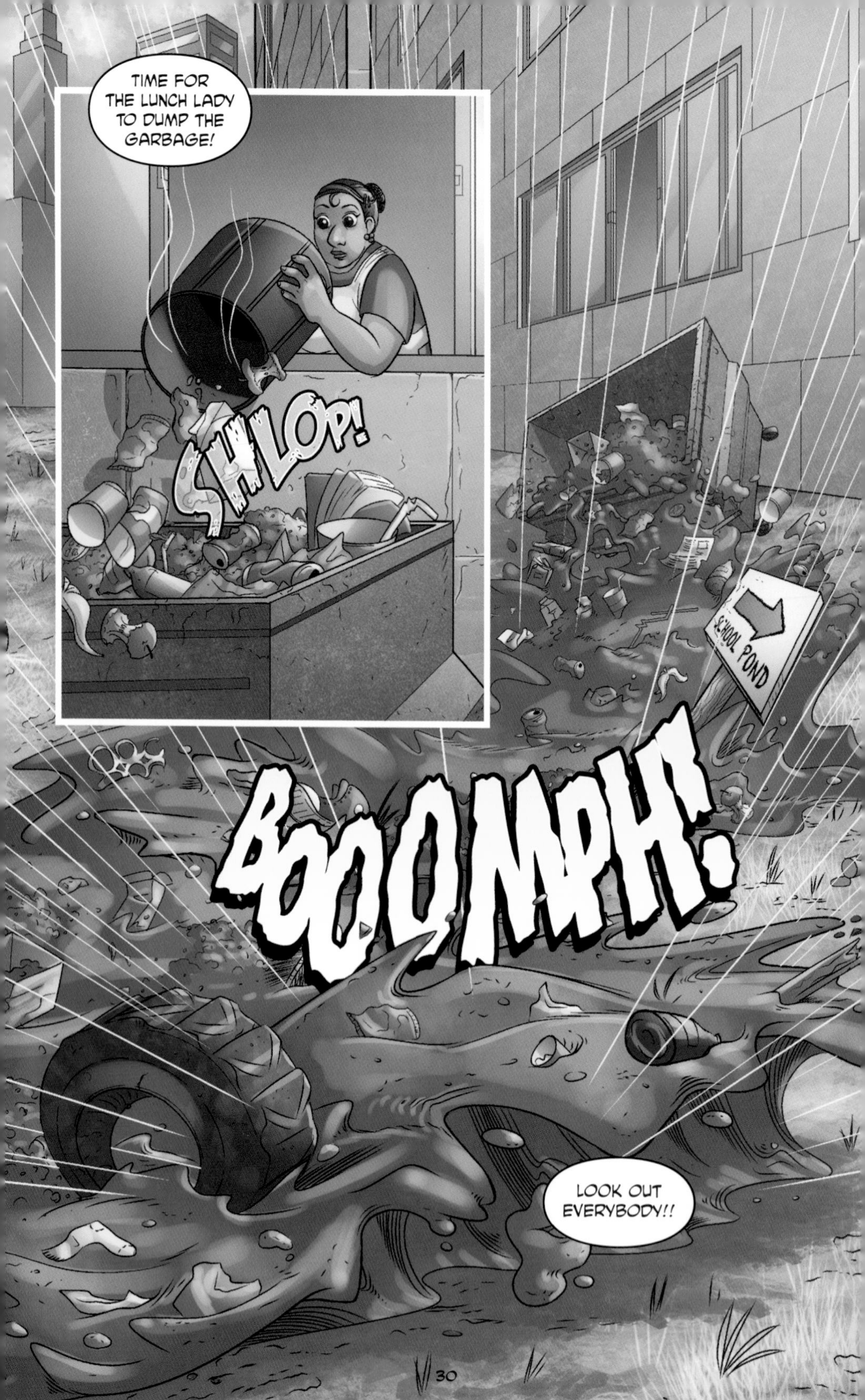
TIME FOR THE LUNCH LADY TO DUMP THE GARBAGE!
SHLOP!
SCHOOL POND
BOOOMPH!
LOOK OUT EVERYBODY!!

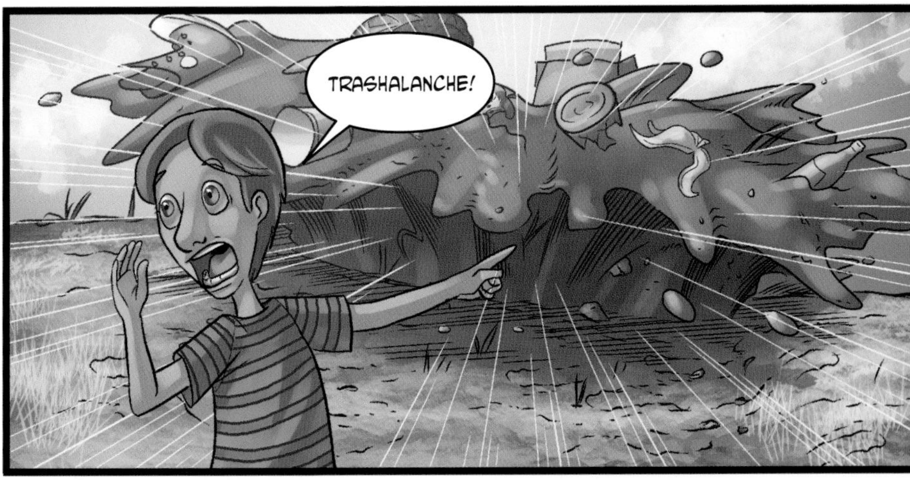
TRASHALANCHE!

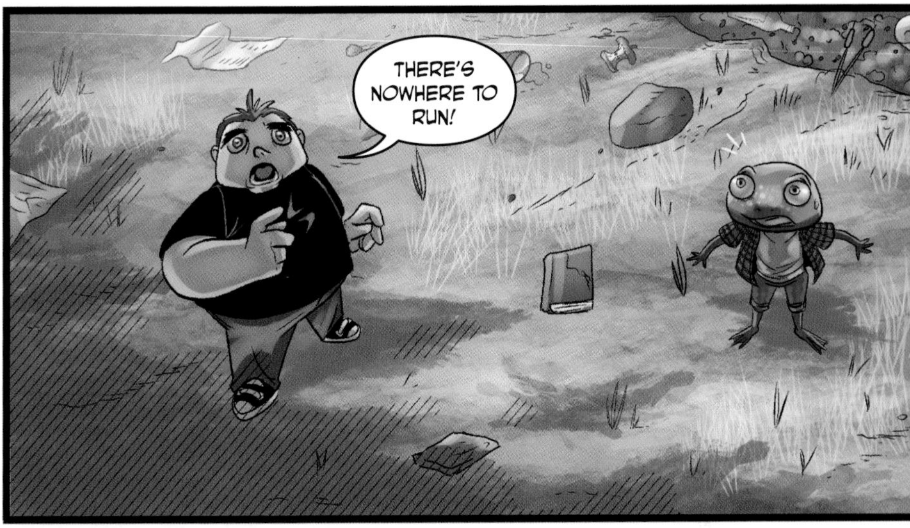
THERE'S NOWHERE TO RUN!

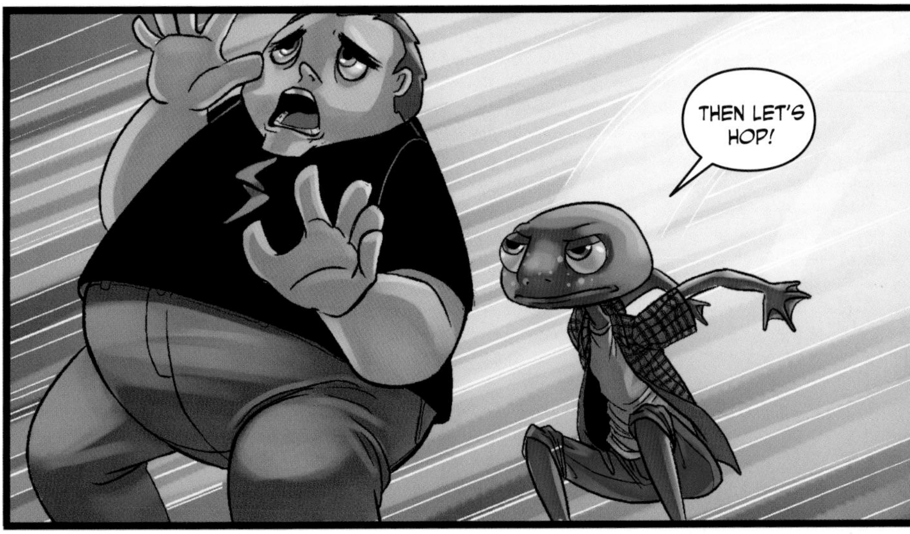
THEN LET'S HOP!

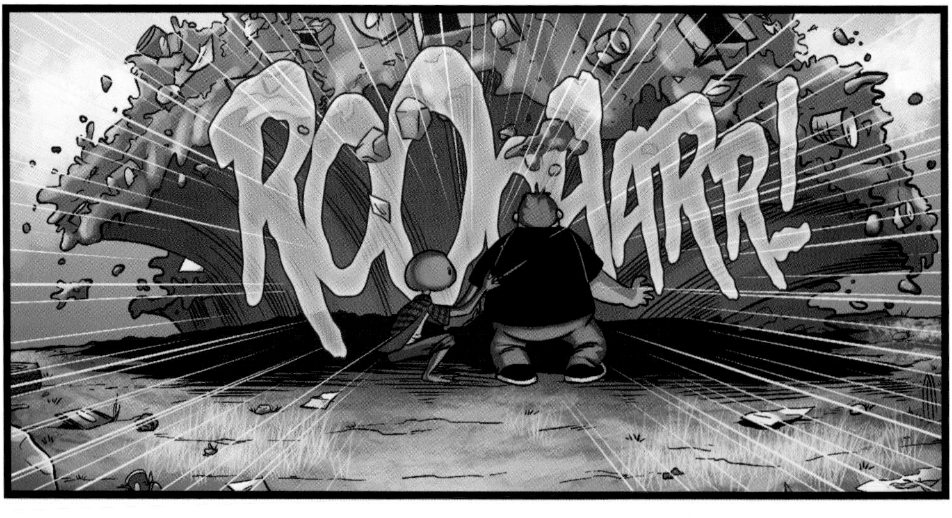
ROOAARR!

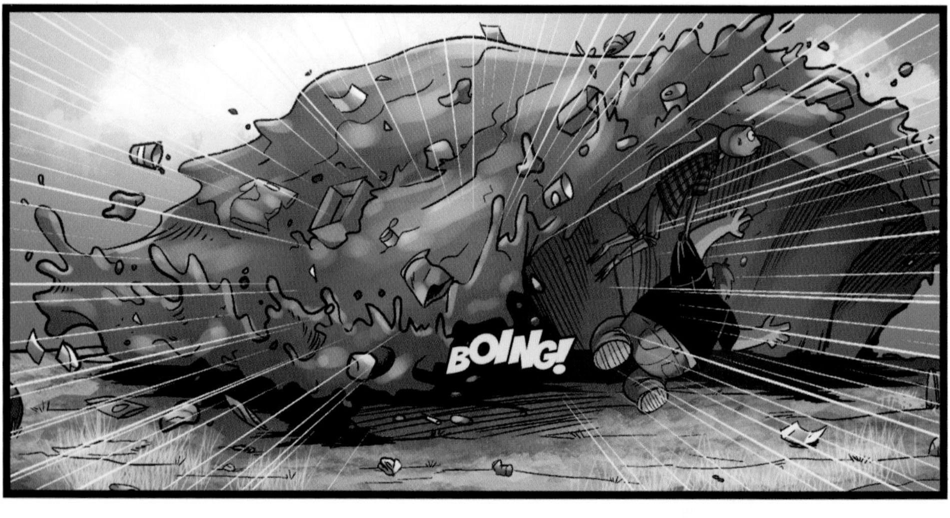
BOING!

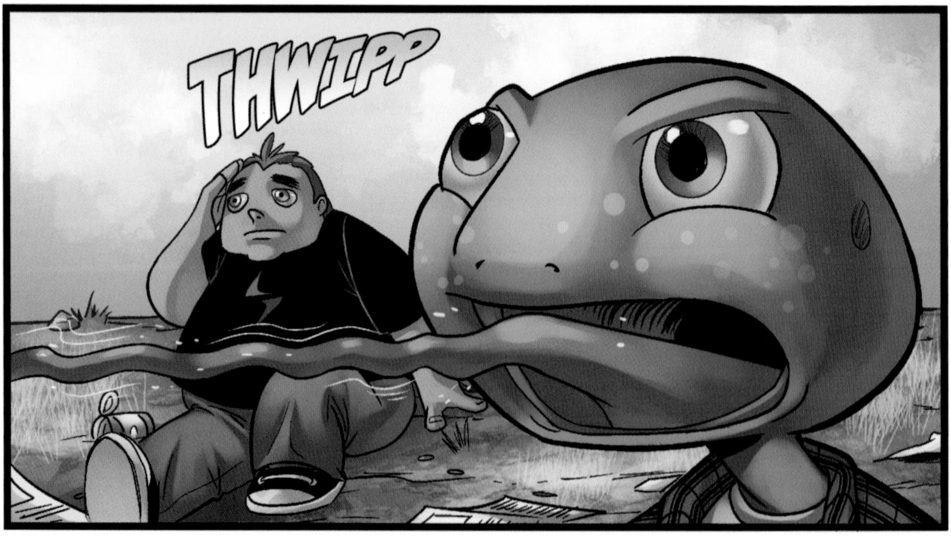
THWIPP

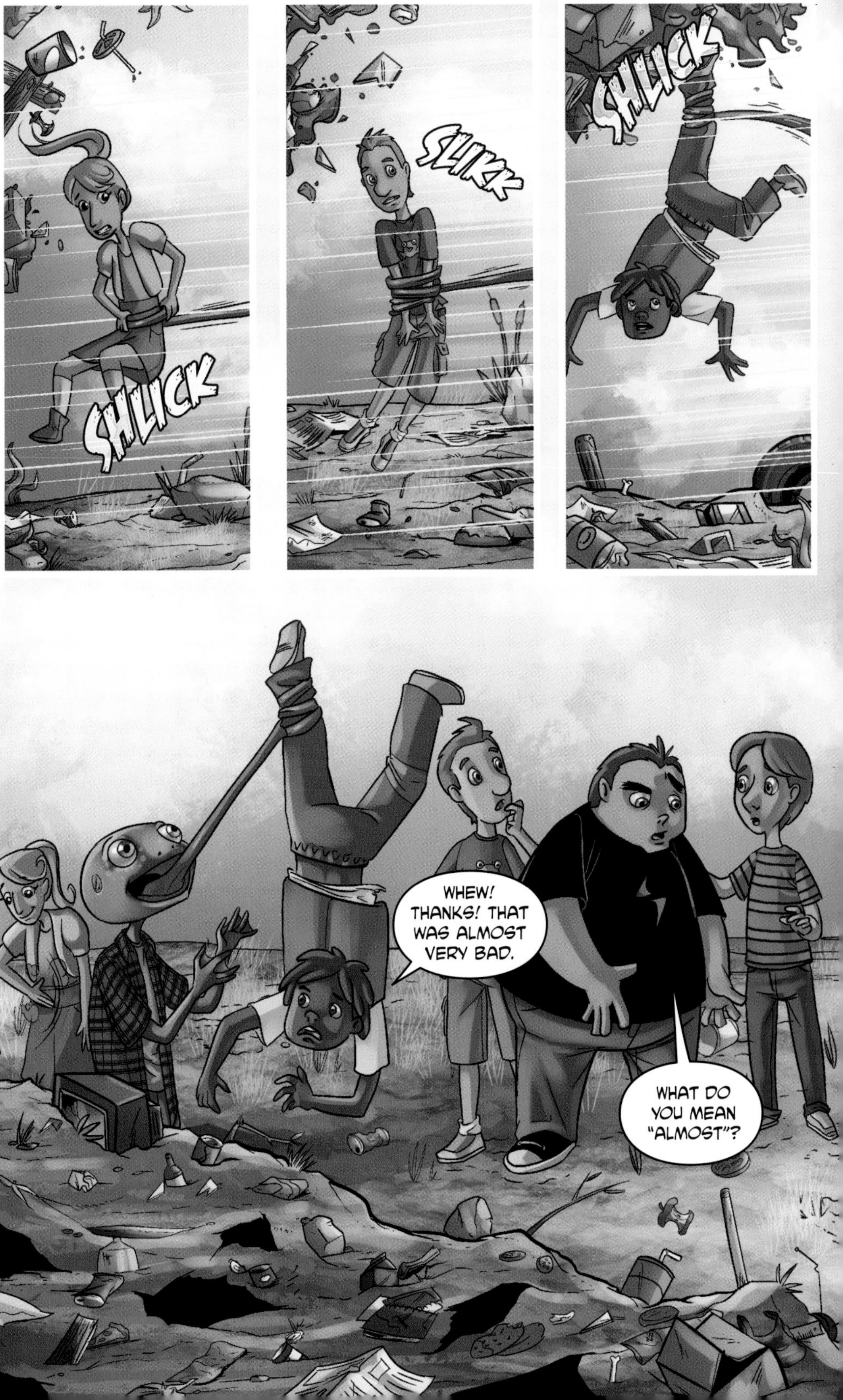
SHLICK
SLIKK
SHLICK
WHEW! THANKS! THAT WAS ALMOST VERY BAD.
WHAT DO YOU MEAN "ALMOST"?

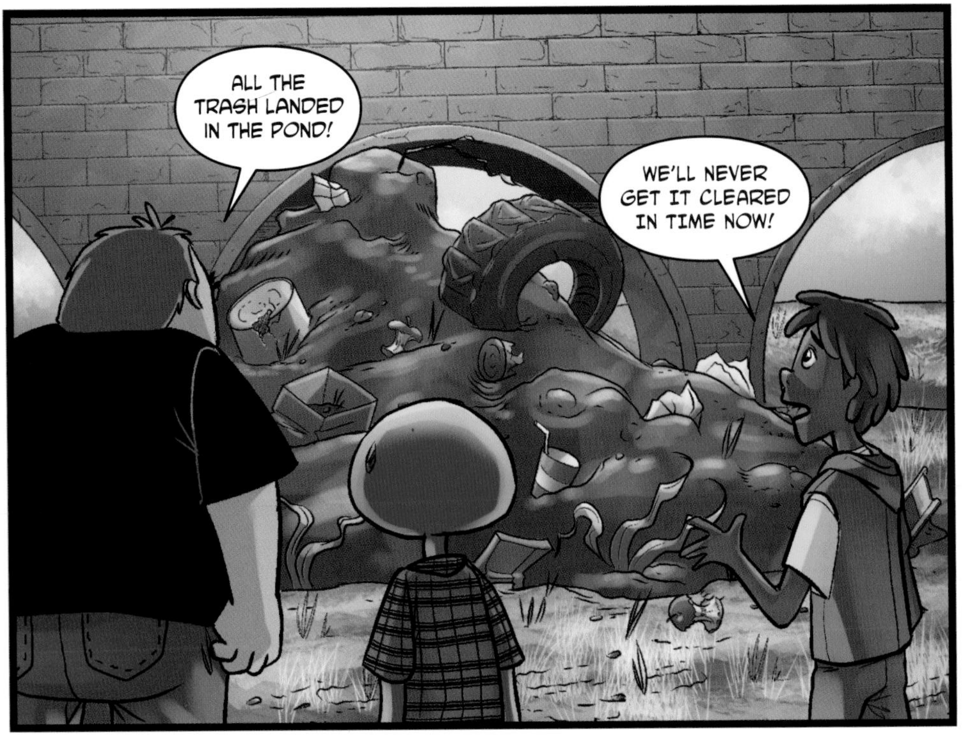
ALL THE TRASH LANDED IN THE POND!
WE'LL NEVER GET IT CLEARED IN TIME NOW!

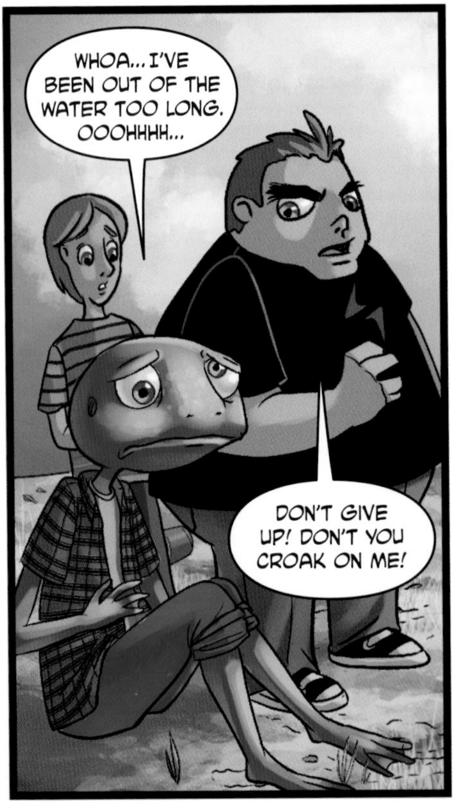
WHOA... I'VE BEEN OUT OF THE WATER TOO LONG. OOOHHHH...
DON'T GIVE UP! DON'T YOU CROAK ON ME!

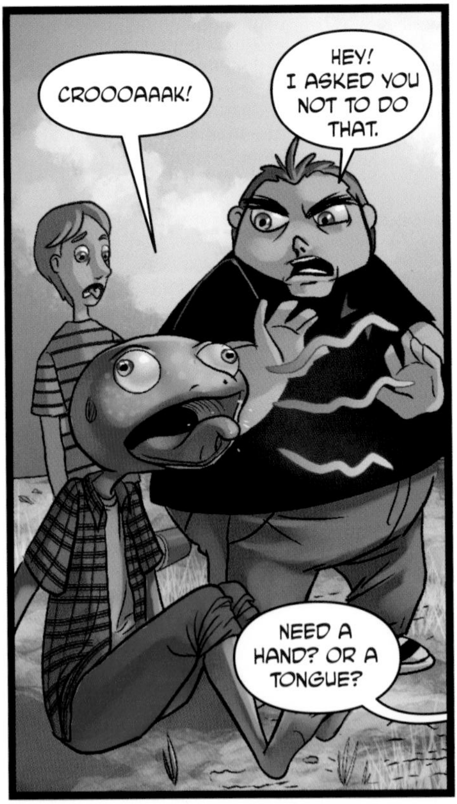
CROOOAAAK!
HEY! I ASKED YOU NOT TO DO THAT.
NEED A HAND? OR A TONGUE?

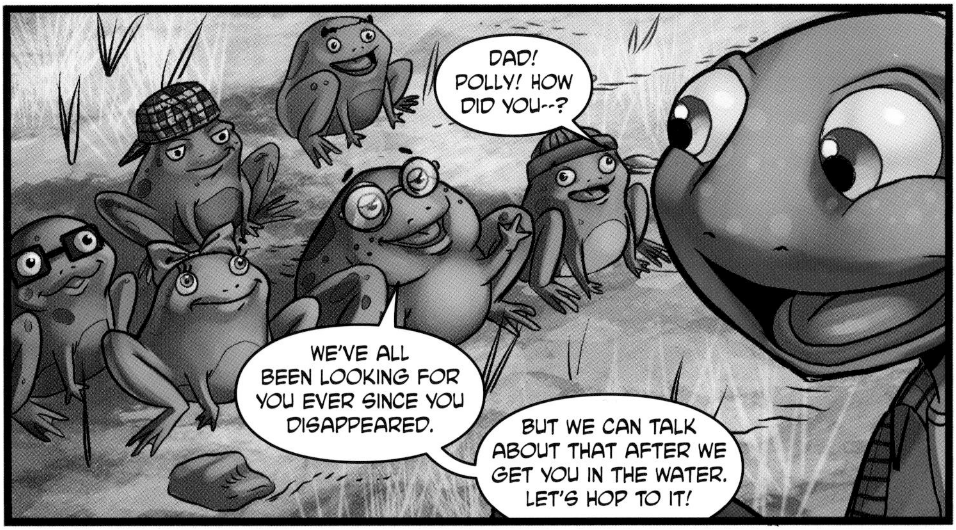
DAD! POLLY! HOW DID YOU--?
WE'VE ALL BEEN LOOKING FOR YOU EVER SINCE YOU DISAPPEARED.
BUT WE CAN TALK ABOUT THAT AFTER WE GET YOU IN THE WATER. LET'S HOP TO IT!

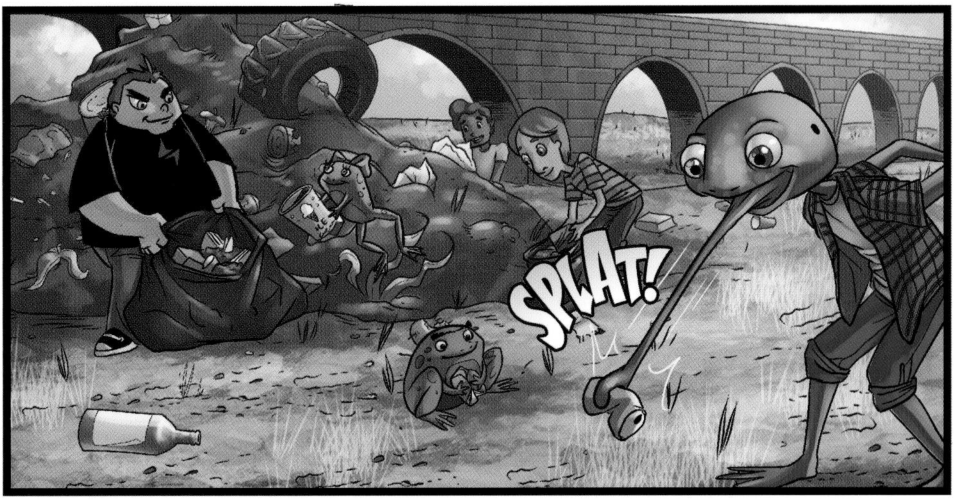
SPLAT!

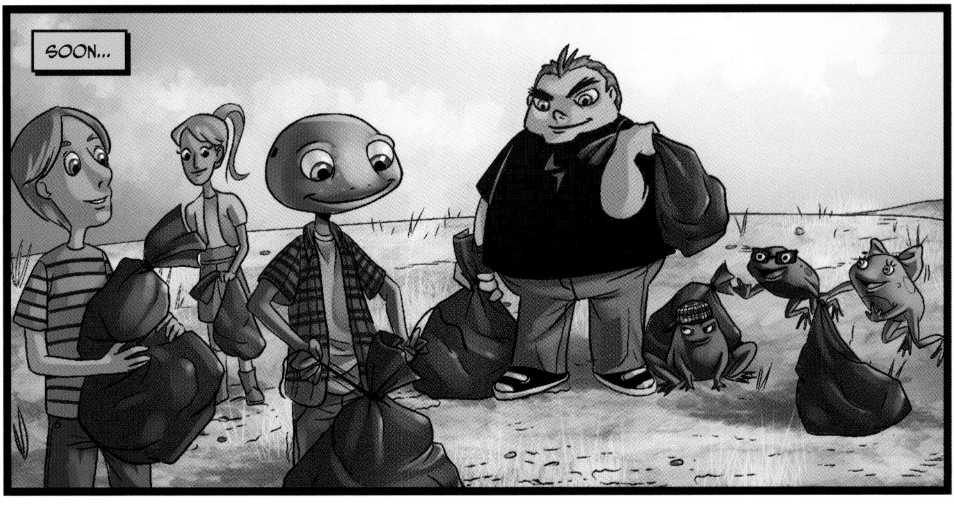
SOON...

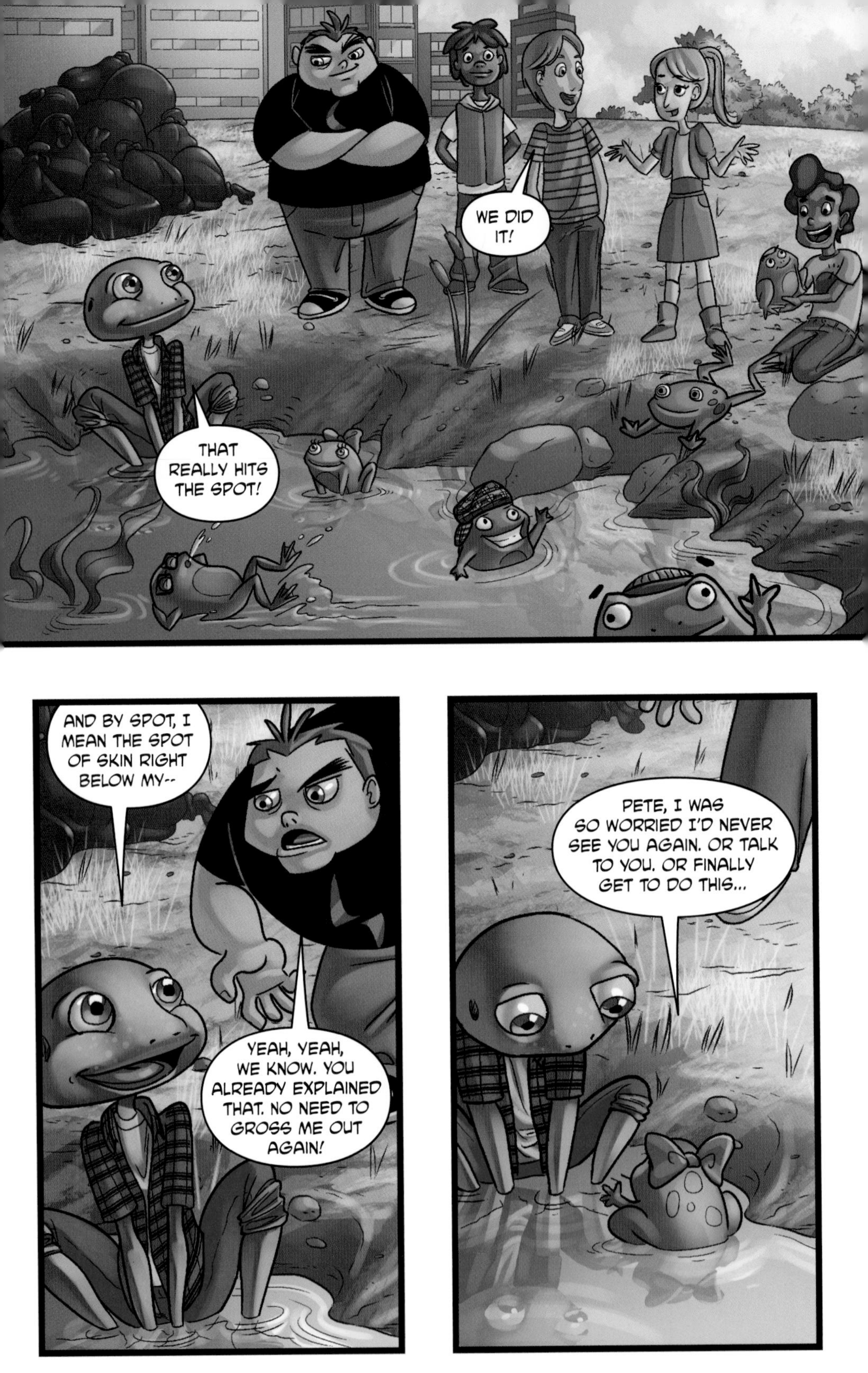
WE DID IT!
THAT REALLY HITS THE SPOT!
AND BY SPOT, I MEAN THE SPOT OF SKIN RIGHT BELOW MY--
YEAH, YEAH, WE KNOW. YOU ALREADY EXPLAINED THAT. NO NEED TO GROSS ME OUT AGAIN!
PETE, I WAS SO WORRIED I'D NEVER SEE YOU AGAIN. OR TALK TO YOU. OR FINALLY GET TO DO THIS...

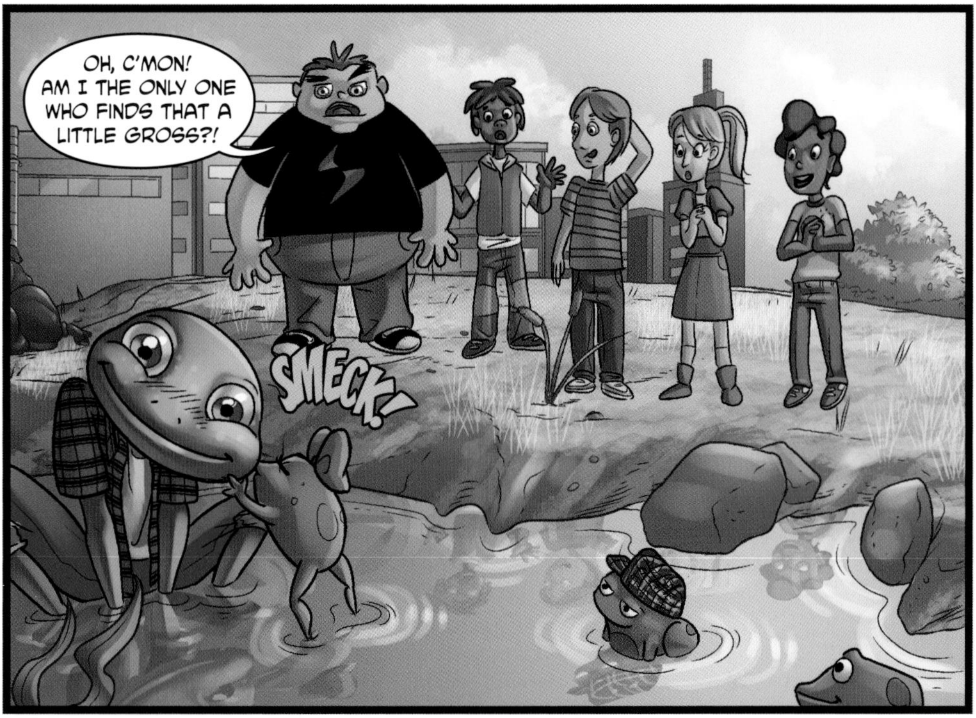
OH, C'MON! AM I THE ONLY ONE WHO FINDS THAT A LITTLE GROSS?!
SMECK!

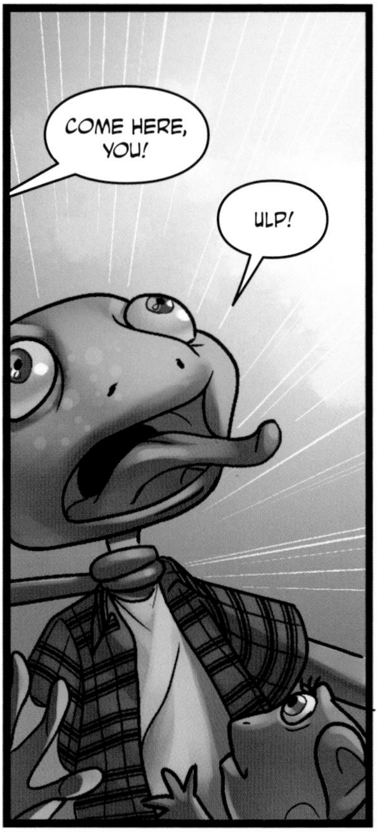
COME HERE, YOU!
ULP!

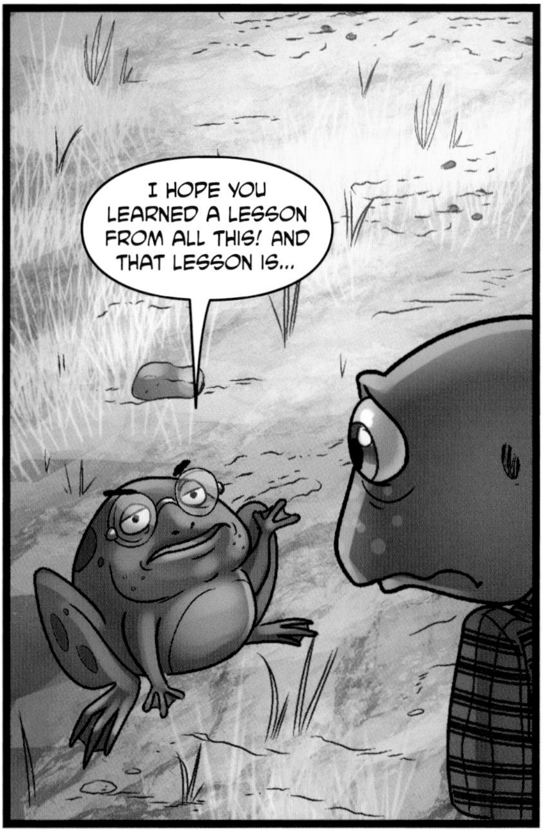
I HOPE YOU LEARNED A LESSON FROM ALL THIS! AND THAT LESSON IS...

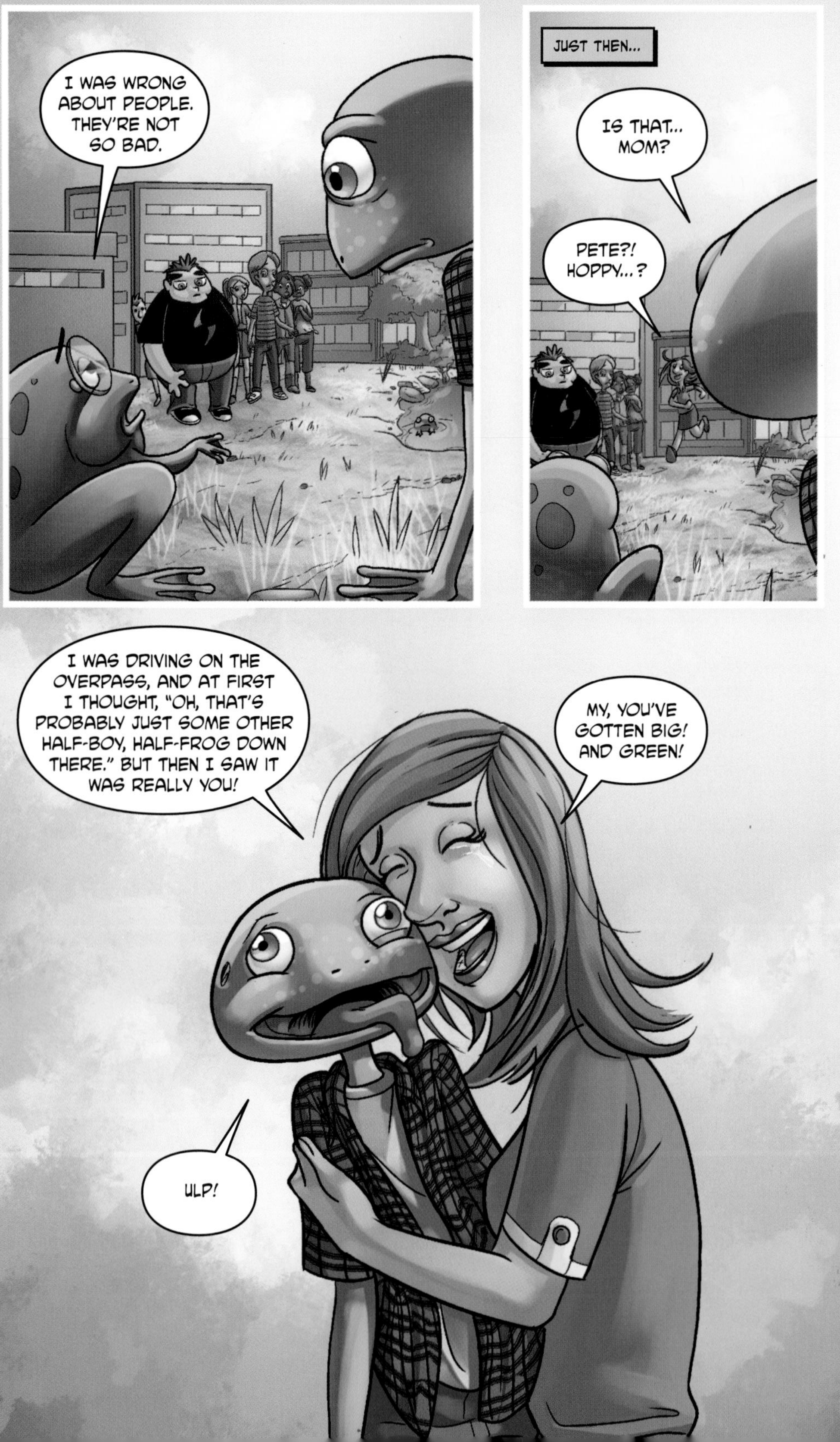
I WAS WRONG ABOUT PEOPLE. THEY'RE NOT SO BAD.
JUST THEN...
IS THAT... MOM?
PETE?! HOPPY...?
I WAS DRIVING ON THE OVERPASS, AND AT FIRST I THOUGHT, "OH, THAT'S PROBABLY JUST SOME OTHER HALF-BOY, HALF-FROG DOWN THERE." BUT THEN I SAW IT WAS REALLY YOU!
MY, YOU'VE GOTTEN BIG! AND GREEN!
ULP!

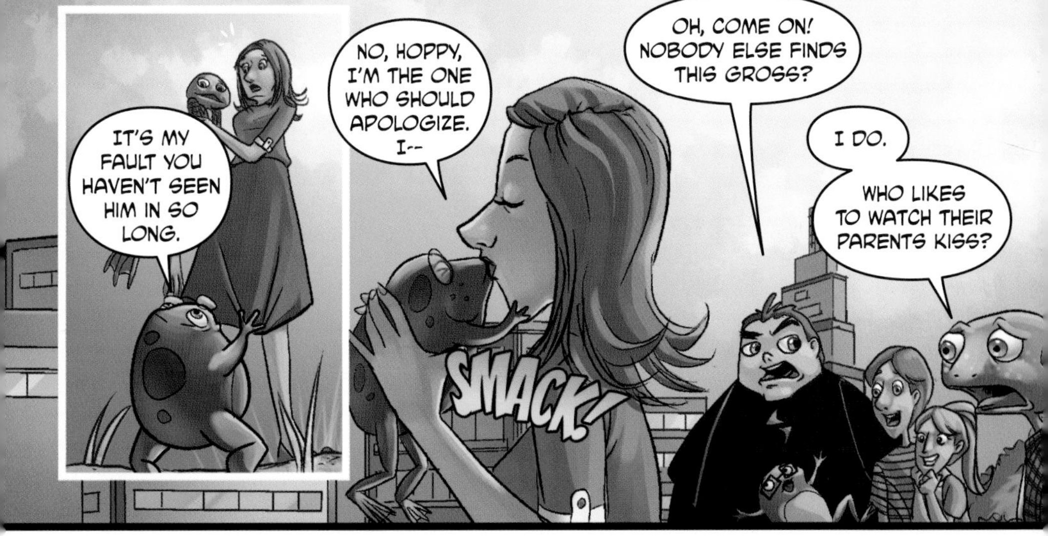
IT'S MY FAULT YOU HAVEN'T SEEN HIM IN SO LONG.
NO, HOPPY, I'M THE ONE WHO SHOULD APOLOGIZE. I--
SMACK!
OH, COME ON! NOBODY ELSE FINDS THIS GROSS?
I DO.
WHO LIKES TO WATCH THEIR PARENTS KISS?

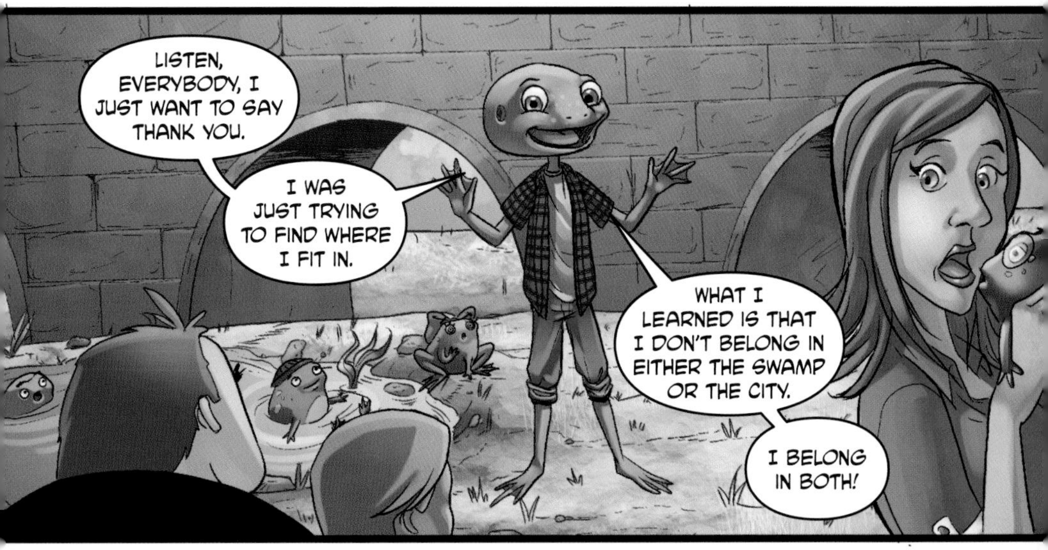
LISTEN, EVERYBODY, I JUST WANT TO SAY THANK YOU.
I WAS JUST TRYING TO FIND WHERE I FIT IN.
WHAT I LEARNED IS THAT I DON'T BELONG IN EITHER THE SWAMP OR THE CITY.
I BELONG IN BOTH!

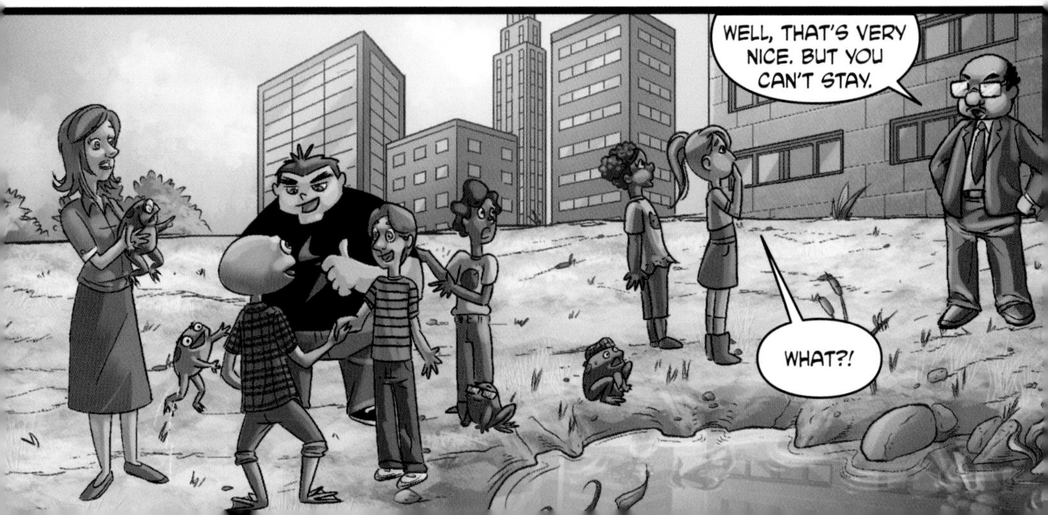
WELL, THAT'S VERY NICE. BUT YOU CAN'T STAY.
WHAT?!

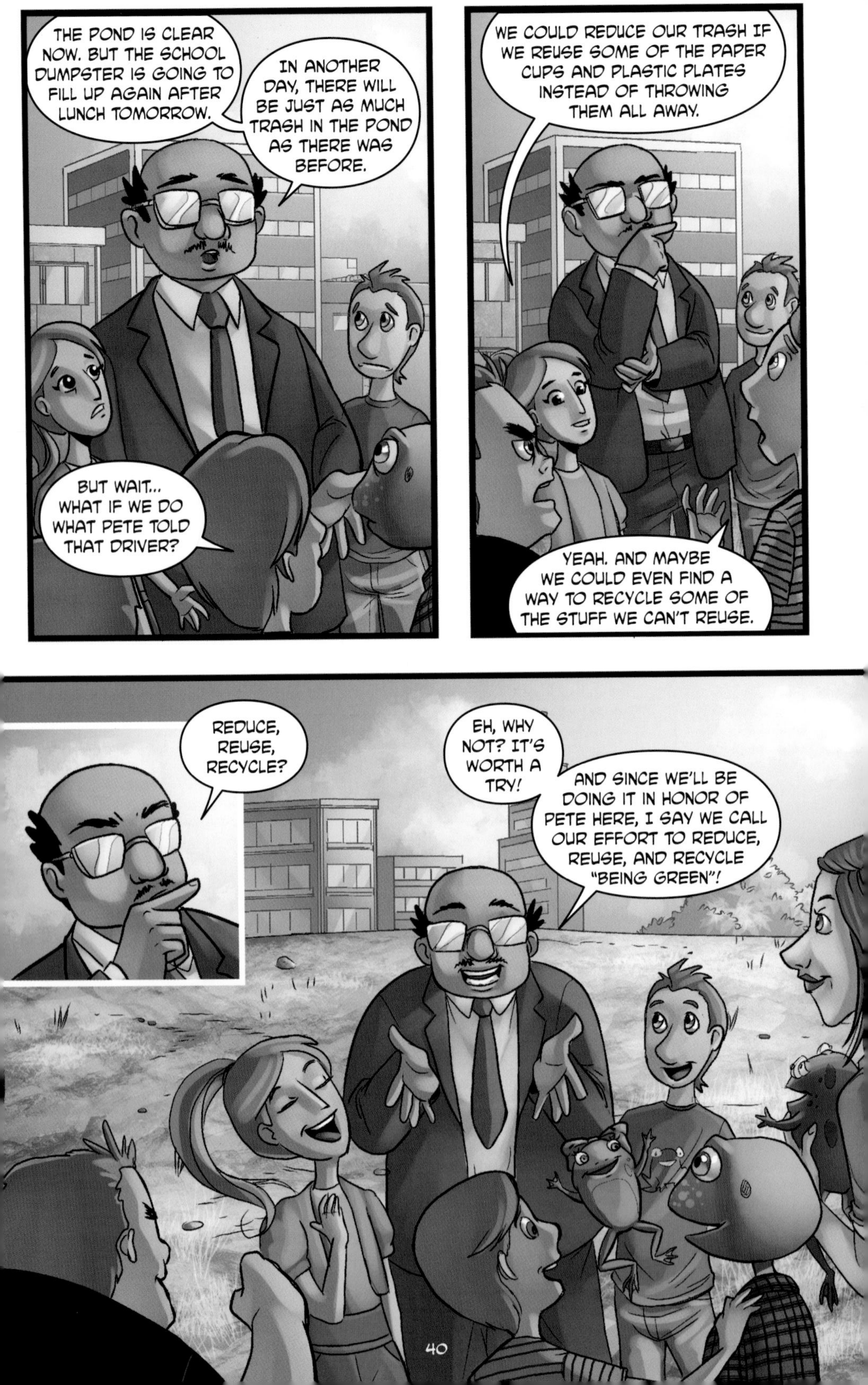
THE POND IS CLEAR NOW. BUT THE SCHOOL DUMPSTER IS GOING TO FILL UP AGAIN AFTER LUNCH TOMORROW.
IN ANOTHER DAY, THERE WILL BE JUST AS MUCH TRASH IN THE POND AS THERE WAS BEFORE.
BUT WAIT... WHAT IF WE DO WHAT PETE TOLD THAT DRIVER?
WE COULD REDUCE OUR TRASH IF WE REUSE SOME OF THE PAPER CUPS AND PLASTIC PLATES INSTEAD OF THROWING THEM ALL AWAY.
YEAH. AND MAYBE WE COULD EVEN FIND A WAY TO RECYCLE SOME OF THE STUFF WE CAN'T REUSE.
REDUCE, REUSE, RECYCLE?
EH, WHY NOT? IT'S WORTH A TRY!
AND SINCE WE'LL BE DOING IT IN HONOR OF PETE HERE, I SAY WE CALL OUR EFFORT TO REDUCE, REUSE, AND RECYCLE "BEING GREEN"!

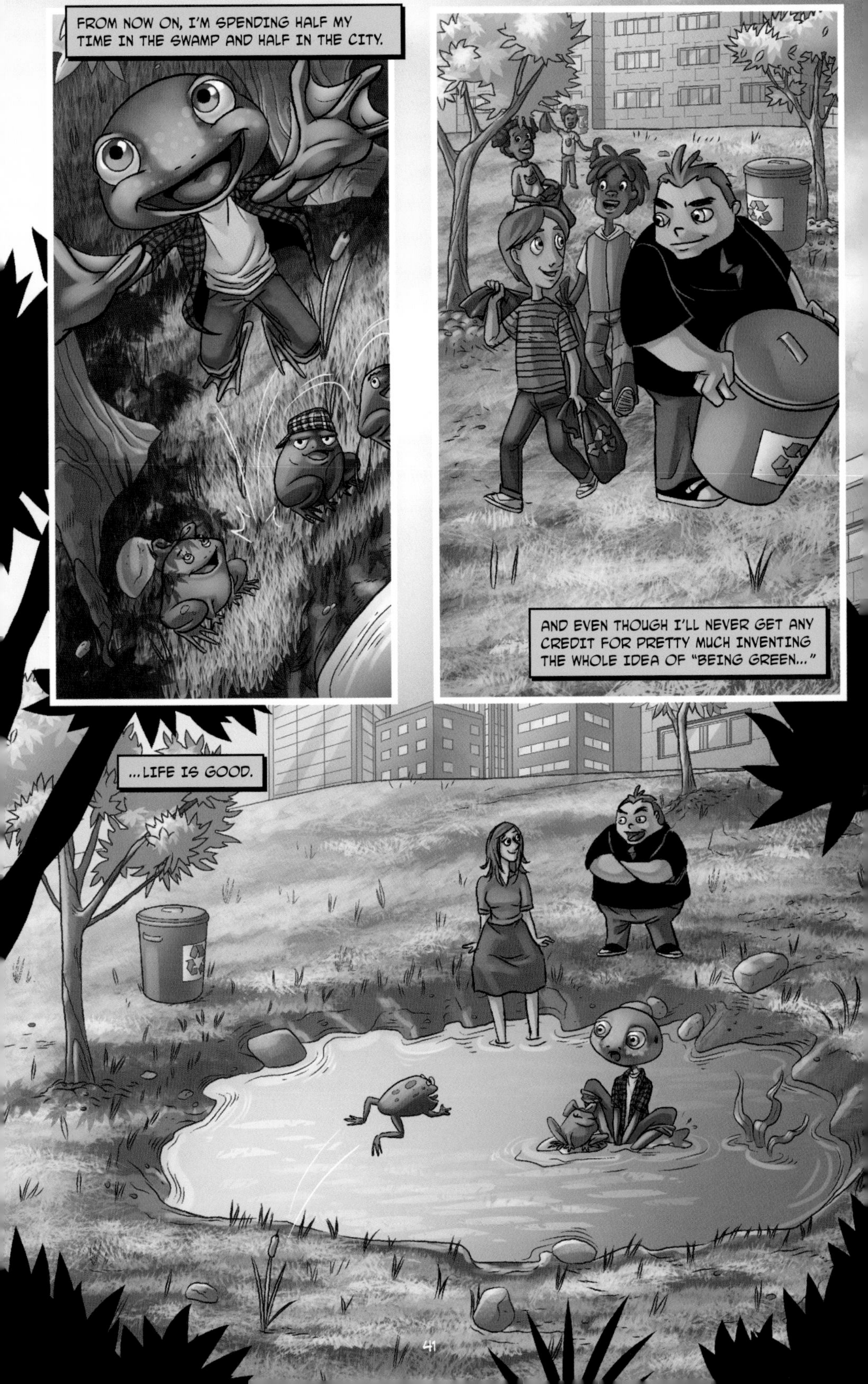
FROM NOW ON, I'M SPENDING HALF MY TIME IN THE SWAMP AND HALF IN THE CITY.
AND EVEN THOUGH I'LL NEVER GET ANY CREDIT FOR PRETTY MUCH INVENTING THE WHOLE IDEA OF "BEING GREEN..."
...LIFE IS GOOD.

CREATORS

SCOTT SONNEBORN

Scott Sonneborn has written many books, one circus (for Ringling Bros. Barnum & Bailey), and a bunch of TV shows. He's been nominated for one Emmy and spent three very cool years working at DC Comics. He lives in Los Angeles with his wife and their two sons.

SERGIO MARTÍNEZ

Sergio Martinez was born in Monterrey, Mexico. He has enjoyed drawing since before he can remember. After graduating from the Visual Arts Faculty in the UANL, he began working as a background designer and illustrator for Luciernaga Studio. He is also a comic artist for Graphikslava Studio, drawing comics for IDW, Marvel Comics, DC Comics, and Stone Arch Books.

ANGÉLICA BRACHO

Angelica Bracho was born in Monterrey, Mexico, where she studied Visual Arts. Angelica has colaborated with Graphikslava Studio, coloring and drawing comics for publishers like IDW, Marvel, DC, and Stone Arch Books.

GLOSSARY

absorb (ab-ZORB)—to take in or suck or swallow up

amphibian (am-FIB-ee-uhn)—a cold-blooded animal that breathes with gills when young, but develops lungs and lives on land as an adult, such as frogs, toads, and salamanders

clumsy (KLUHM-zee)—lacking skill or grace in movement

curious (KYUR-ee-uhss)—eager to find out something

jealous (JEL-uhss)—wanting something another person has

obvious (OB-vee-uhss)—easy to see or understand

recycle (ree-SYE-kuhl)—to process (liquid body waste, glass, or cans) in order to regain materials for human use

reduce (ri-DOOSS)—to make something smaller or less

tadpole (TAD-pole)—the larva of a frog that has a rounded body and a long tail, breathes with gills, and lives in water

VISUAL QUESTIONS

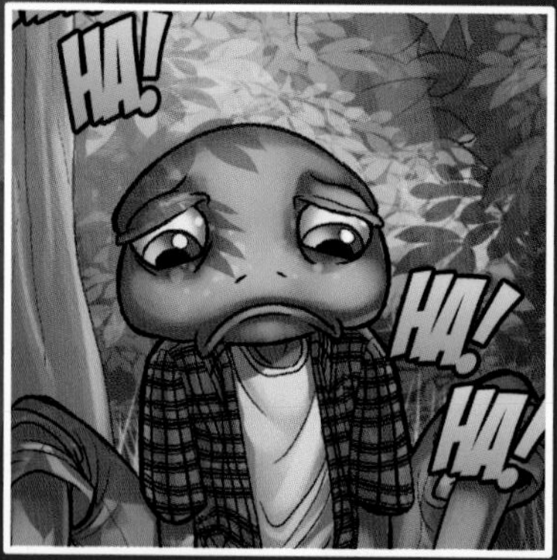
HA!
HA!
HA!

1. The way a character's eyes and mouth are illustrated can tell a lot about the emotions he or she is feeling. How do you think Pete Bogg is feeling in the panel at left (from page 11)? Describe how you can tell.

2. On page 19, the artist illustrates Pete Bogg's thoughts with a comic book element called a "thought bubble". Describe another way you could show or tell what a character is thinking.

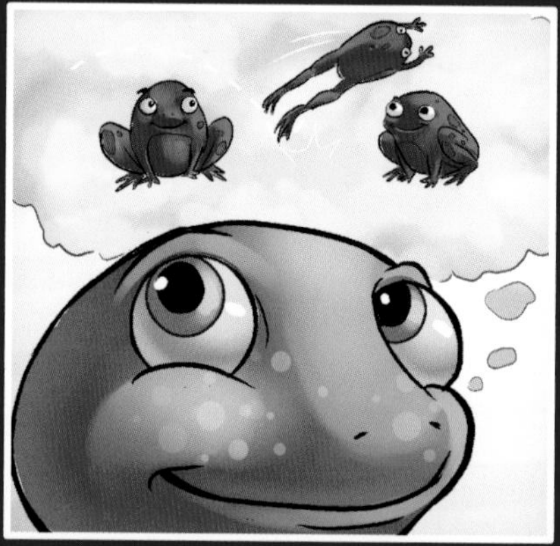

3. In comics, sound effects (also known as SFX) are used to show sounds. Make a list of all the sound effects in this book, and then write a definition for each term. Soon, you'll have your own SFX dictionary!

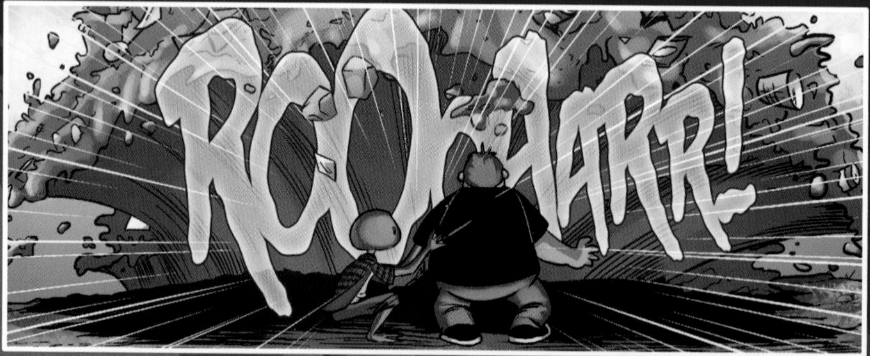
ROOWARR!

4. Pete Bogg is half human and half frog. In what ways is he like a frog? In what ways is he like a human? Explain your answers using examples from the story.

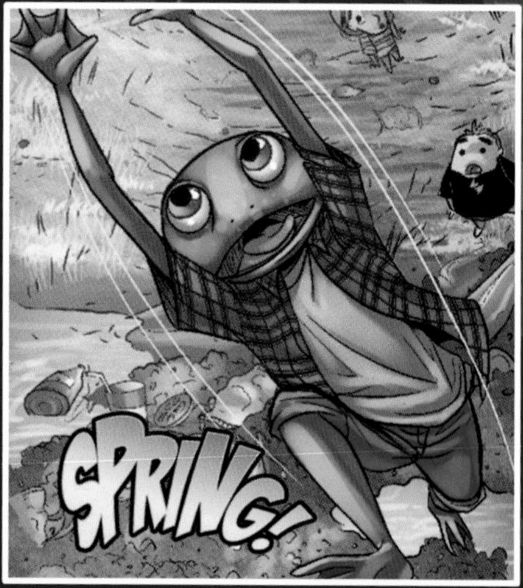
SPRING!

5. Pete Bogg found ways to improve his environment by reducing, reusing, and recycling. What are some ways you can improve your own environment each day?

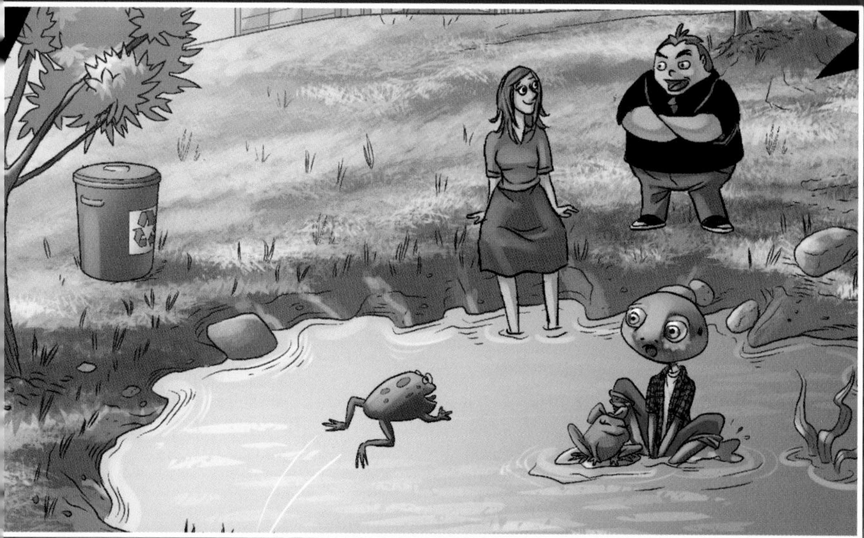

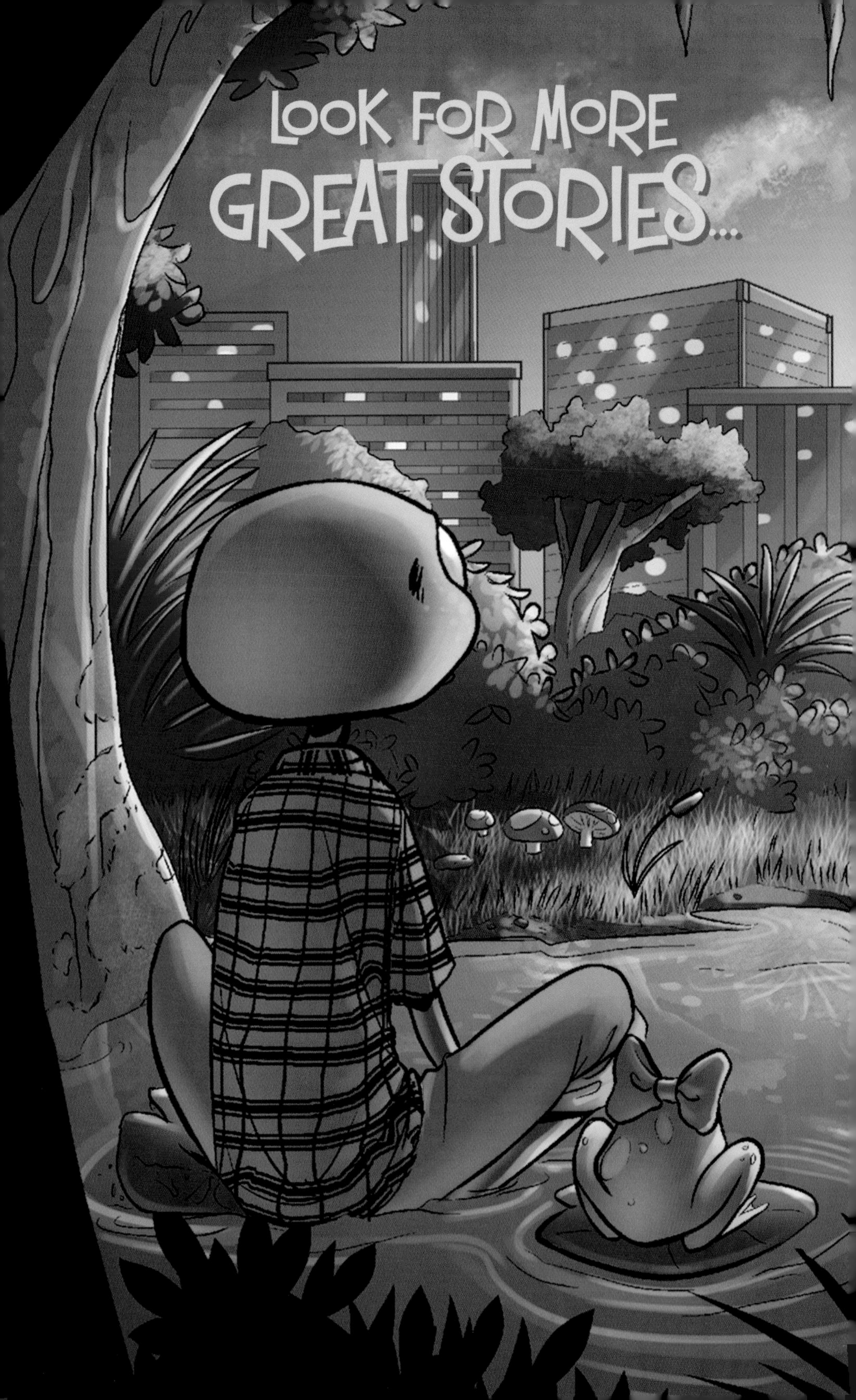
LOOK FOR MORE
GREAT STORIES...

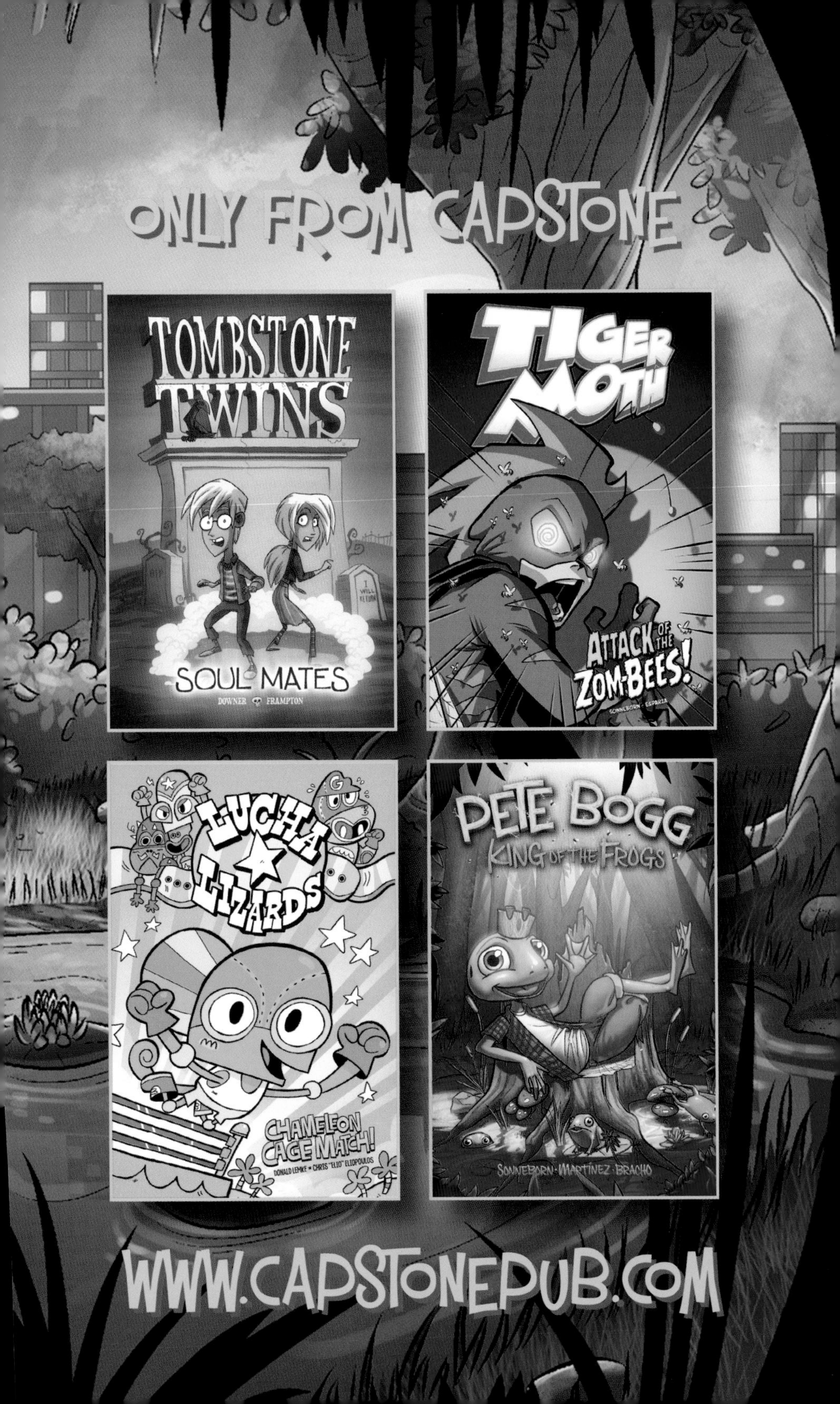

ONLY FROM CAPSTONE
TOMBSTONE TWINS
SOUL MATES
DOWNER FRAMPTON
TIGER MOTH
ATTACK OF THE ZOM-BEES!
SONNEBORN · ESPARZA
LUCHA LIZARDS
CHAMELEON CAGE MATCH!
DONALD LEMKE ★ CHRIS "ELIO" ELIOPOULOS
PETE BOGG
KING OF THE FROGS
SONNEBORN · MARTÍNEZ · BRACHO
WWW.CAPSTONEPUB.COM

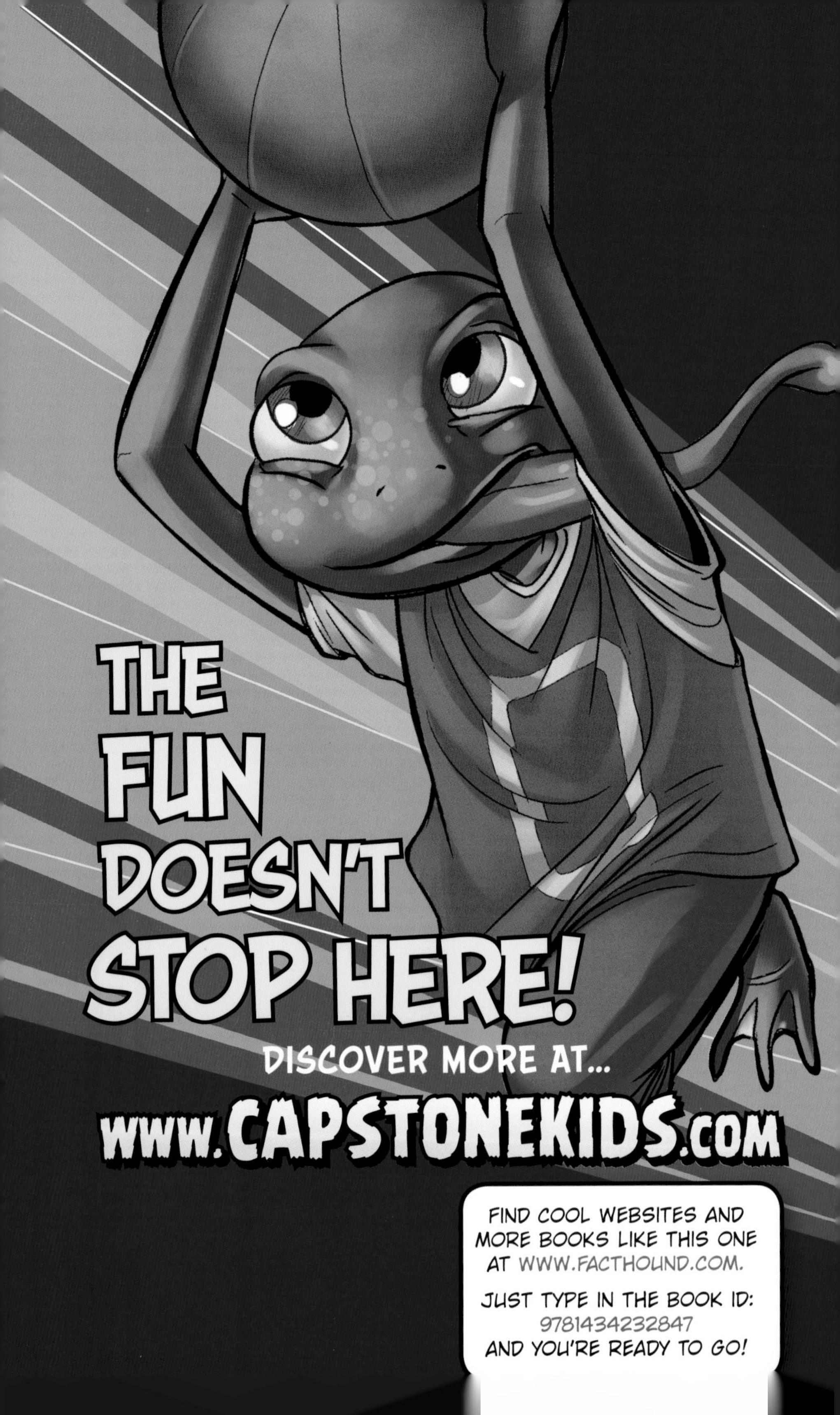
THE FUN DOESN'T STOP HERE!
DISCOVER MORE AT...
www.CAPSTONEKIDS.com
FIND COOL WEBSITES AND MORE BOOKS LIKE THIS ONE AT WWW.FACTHOUND.COM.
JUST TYPE IN THE BOOK ID: 9781434232847 AND YOU'RE READY TO GO!